The Work of Gods

By

Kevin James Donoghue

The Great Book of Alchemy
Part I

A 5th Worlde Saga

1st edition

Dedication

For George; an exceptional son.

Acknowledgement

A special thank you to Martin for his gramatic skills and endless conversation.

A note from the author

The Great Book of Alchemy is collection of sagas of the 5th Worlde. These sagas are not a series of historical novels, and whilst many of the characters have indeed appeared in the history of your world, in the 5th Worlde, their histories are completely different and a substantial amount of imagination has been used to ensure this fact.

The Bells of the Watch

Number of Bells	Bell Pattern	Middle Watch	Morning Watch	Forenoon Watch	After-noon Watch	Dog Watch First	Dog Watch Last	First Watch
one	1	0.30	4.30	8.30	12.30	16.30		20.30
two	2	1.00	5.00	9.00	13.00	17.00		21.00
three	2 1	1.30	5.30	9.30	13.30	17.30		21.30
four	2 2	2.00	6.00	10.00	14.00	18.00		22.00
five	2 2 1	2.30	6.30	10.30	14.30		18.30	22.30
six	2 2 2	3.00	7.00	11.00	15.00		19.00	23.00
seven	2 2 2 1	3.30	7.30	11.30	15.30		19.30	23.30
eight	2 2 2 2	4.00	8.00	12.00	16.00		20.00	24.00

The Work of Gods

1

A Hard Rain

Sir Thomas Devereux; is in his rooms above the emporium of Messrs Camden and Sons, by royal warrant and appointment to his gracious majesty Edward II, Royal Astronomers, Astrologers, Cartographers, Chart Makers, Horologist, Navigators, Oikouménê, Scribists, and who are of The Worshipful Company of Painter-Stainers and Sporting Bookmakers, which are located in Neal's Yard, London, WC2H 9DP.

'The empire stretches across the world map, pink ~ like the blotches on a drunkard's face.'

My quill scratched across the bottom of the parchment, leaving a deep black trail in its wake, and I smiled. My smile is large and often on my boyish face.

'Yes, that is better.' I said.

'Is the room growing dim? Should I light another candle? Do we have another candle to spend?' I asked, as I dropped the quill from my stiff little fingers. It made a small, insignificant clatter on to the mess-strewn table, and I eased back into the soft chair and listened to the hard rain as it pounded against the windowpanes. The rain fell with a rock

steady beat, relentless and rhythmic, and outside it
left huge pools and rivulets in the yard, and there
seemed to be no end to its dance for the foreseeable
future.

'I love the rain, don't you?' I asked Sir Anatole, my
new flatmate. I was suddenly fascinated, hypnotised
by a huge globule of the stuff. It hung ponderously,
like an old hag's breast, a half-pear, with a small dark
nipple. It stuck to the windowpane in the grease and
the dirt, clinging for dear life, yet only momentarily,
before it cascaded downwards and spiralled off and
outwards into the dark oblivion of Neal's Yard, London.

'Do you ever wonder if the raindrops could repre-
sent your life? You know, as if you were falling down
to earth? Just like the smallest piece of sand, that
falls downwards, through the time glass?' I continued.

'I often have the same dream.' I said more softly;

'I am falling, as if from the grace of the gods. Falling from heaven. Spiralling like a raindrop. Ever
downwards…into the seventh circle of hell. Do you
think life is really like that?' I asked.

Sir Anatole de Sourisblanche did not answer. He
did not say a word. He just arched an eyebrow and
looked at me quizzically with his dark sullen eyes. He
shook his head slowly from side to side, as he stroked
his heavy moustache. He looked like an old father
regarding a favoured but idiot son.

'I remember John saying that;

'Our souls float from one world to another.'

Now for those of you who don't know John… John
Dee is my old teacher and mentor.

'You don't know John do you?' I enquired of Sir
Anatole.

'You know, the druids preach a similar ideology. I
believe they call it…transmigrating.'

Anatole walked across the room with a quick, quirky, little, gait and settled on the cushions at the edge of my bed.

'And,' I continued, ignoring the fact that he was ignoring me;

'And I often wonder, what if that one moment's pause, on the windowpane of the world, was in fact the high point of my life. What would life be worth then?'

'Oh,' I sighed,

'John would know.' I looked at him and watched as he scratched his head and then his ear.

'What was that song he sang last week? When we were downing a few tankards in the Strangled Cat?' I mused.

The Strangled Cat is one of London Town's famous drinking emporiums. It is hidden in the depths of Soho. John, or to give him his proper title, Doctor Dee, is considered to be a handsome man. He is tall, and slender, with a very fair, sanguine, complexion and he has a fine beard, which is as white as milk, and is at least three times longer than my member, even upon the very warmest of days. He is for ever tutoring and counselling the nobles of the realm; He is a King's man, without any doubt. And many consider him to be the embodiment of the enlightened man; '*The soul of his age.*'

My mother's cousin, Bess Tudor, has been his student since she crawled out of the cradle. She is one who receives his esteemed council upon a daily basis. I believe that he also has been consulted by that wild brood of Henry FitzEmpress, the King's cousins, who hail from somewhere sunny in the Old Possessions; Anjou, I believe.

'Speaking of Anjou.' I said, even though I hadn't been.

'Have you heard the story about the old chap's

mother? You remember that she is Matilda of England of course - the Holy Roman Empress. Well...' I paused like you do when you're getting ready to tell a really good tale;

'Well, it's about her and the Archer of Salford, as they called him.' I stretched out the words in a soft whisper, to emphasise the salaciousness of the remark.

'Let's face it, the lady is quite the merry little widow, and how not?' I took a breath.

'When she was just a mere girl, of twelve or so, they married her off to some old greybeard. He died after about ten years and she was left a widow at the age of twenty and two. And then, her family married her off again, this time to a thirteen-year-old boy. Can you imagine that? It must have had some effect on her as she became simply notorious...Oh the tales. But then again, what do you expect from an Angevin?' I took another, longer breath.

'Her mother, Adelaide Blanche, saw off five husbands you know. I guess that she must have simply worn them out.'

'Anyway, about John...as I was saying, in the evenings, he studies the skies and the paths and movements of the stars and the planets. Some say that he teraffics in the dark arts. That he speaks with the angels and demons. To be honest with you, it is not something that we have ever spoken about. In fact, it all sounds rather rummy to me. What do you think?'

Sir Anatole picked his nose with the end of his stubby little finger and swallowed the resulting prize without a moment's hesitation, and after only the most cursory of glances. I continued, ignoring my roommate's après midnight feast.

'No...well I am of the opinion that John is the wisest of men; and both my parents dislike him immensely. You know, it was at the recommendation of the Earl of Leicester that John first became my tutor when I was up at Cambridge. I think someone at Pembroke must have had a fit or something…after what I have always thought of as a miracle, they admitted me. I suppose that large amounts of money must have changed hands. Dr Dee is himself, predictably, a John's man. However, father - have you met father, no? Well father, he is the Earl of Essex you know; he soon put an end to that scenario.'

'Mother's dislike of John came later. I'm not sure why they fell out. I think it had something to do with cousin Bess, and the succession.' I stretched and continue to watch the rain fall for a few more moments.

'John and I have always been friendly. Sometimes, to be honest with you, I wonder what it is that he really sees in me - after all, I'm a notoriously fickle, lazy and irrelevant sort of chap, or so my family claim. But he does seem to like the books I create… just to supplement the handouts from the mater you know, and he also seems to enjoy my music; and of course my bawdy company.

'Speaking of handouts…you are aware that the rent is due next week?' I reminded him with a meaningful look. You have to break these new chaps in quickly nowadays or they simply take advantage.

'We often meet in the squalor that is Wardour Street, and drink a tankard or two as we watch the various minstrels. He is a very adept performer himself you know. Oh yes. I remember the song now. It was one of the old classics, performed by the famous Stomping Mandolins, it's called *Sweet, Sweet Dreams.*'

And picking up my lute, I strummed the opening chords and started to sing softly to myself, as I looked out of the window into the dark, wet night.

All life is but a fleeting dream,
The smallest dram is tempting,
So take a swig,
When 'ere ye can,
Of death you will have plenty…

And when the jug is empty,
We float away and die,
And when the jug is em - m - pty,

Sweet…sweet dreams,
Will float on by….

Suddenly the candles guttered and a cold gust blew down the chimney. It swirled about the room, billowing the window hangings and scattering my parchments. And I felt the distinct chill of winter's breath on my cheek for the first time this year. It was then that *Red Feather*, my curved steel Ottoman sword, a lethal edged scimitar, and a sad reminder of my ill-fated crusade, began to rattle fiercely, before falling from where it hung. It clattered on the chess table dislodging the white king.

There was a scent of jasmine. I felt my ears pop and, just for a moment, from the very corner of my eye I caught a glimpse of the Jinn. It darted across the room. A strange collection of translucent light. When I looked again…it was gone. It had completely vanished, like they always do. It was the strangest sensation, one that brought with it a sense of impending doom. Once again I became distinctly aware of my own mortality.

'Did you just see that? Did you see it? The Jinn? A

messenger from the gods. Did you see it?' I asked Sir Anatole. He shrugged his shoulders. Them scratched his cock and picked at his nose again.

I bent to collect Red Feather. The sword felt comfortable and warm in my hand. I unsheathed her and ran through a quinte parry, then a riposte, and counter -riposte.

The early hours of the morning had crept upon us. A miserable and melancholy time I always find. Foolishly I had let the fire burn down low. Now only the last embers remained to warm the room. I pulled at my heavy robe, making it tighter around my waist, before lifting it high up on to my shoulders and tugging at it snugly around the back of my neck. I quickly tied the cord, fastening it around my still youthful body. The woollen morning star which was attached to the top of my nightcap, dangled freely and bounced against my face and I casually chewed at it. It's a bad habit, I know, but one that always gives me a soft comfort.

'Winter has brought his grace a hard reign, and the stench of war hangs over England's green and pleasant pastures, like a devil befouled petrichor.' I said replacing Red Feather on her mounting. Sir Anatole de Sourisblanche was silent, sullen, moody, and as unresponsive as ever;

What a mardy bum.

2

The Call To Deveroux House

Sir Thomas Devereux; is in his rooms above the emporium of Messrs Camden and Sons, by royal warrant and appointment to his gracious majesty Edward II, Royal Astronomers, Astrologers, Cartographers, Chart Makers, Horologist, Navigators, Oikouménê, Scribists, and who are of the Worshipful Company of Painter-Stainers and Sporting Bookmakers, which are located in Neal's Yard, London. WC2H 9DP

I rose wearily from my scribing table and made my way across the room. I rolled up my sleeves, placed some kindling on the fire and waited for it to take before adding a few small quartered logs to the growing flames. The leaping tongues of orange, red, and yellow licked around the edges of the wood. I watched the flames closely. It seemed as if a battle raged within the flames, red and yellow armies charged and wheeled against each other. The damp wood gave off a crackling hiss. It spat violently at the night. A spark flew from the fire and hit my right arm. A small shiver ran along the scar there, where the axe had bitten deep. I sighed wearily and shook the thoughts of battle from my head.

As usual, I was doing anything, and I mean ab-so-lute-ly anything, rather than the task which I had set myself. That task upon which I had commenced so many hours ago. My mind was a struggling mass of opposing ideas and I found it impossible to deal with the problems and the questions that plagued it. I just knew that the smallest, the most meagre speck of dust, in this one moment in time - this instant - was more interesting than the total sum of all my creativity combined. As my great friend, the writer, Marlowe often says;

'It pains me so, this art of mine.'

'Sometimes my life seems like an unending struggle. It makes me feel like I am the King of Corinth. You know, the chap with the boulder?' I said to myself, but also to Sir Anatole. This too is a symptom of the age. As the saying went:

'Safer by far to speak to yourself, than to another soul.'

The Inquisitors had their spies everywhere, and nobody, and I do mean absolutely nobody, no matter how high their birth or well connected at court that they may seem, was truly safe from their malevolent clutches. Their reach stretched across the country, a bitter, twisted, thing. Its long sharp talons raked at the very soul of a man. Its ears and eyes were hidden in the open, as well as in the deepest, darkest shadows and their unbridled lust for enforcing these damned new cultural laws was legendary. As John had said;

'Like taking a hammer to an olive.'

I have told you that I am sharing my rooms above the cartographer's emporium and workshop with someone new? Sir Anatole de Sourisblanche, is a small, dark eyed, swarthy creature of a sullen, moody, and unresponsive hue. He is selfish, sulky and preening, and he is forever stroking his whiskers and smoothing down his long, brown, matted hair. In all honesty, I'm not sure I really like the fellow at all but…well, lodgings in London are hard to find, and expensive; even though the family has its connections, and very good they are too, as I'm sure you will recollect. However the money is all my mother's and she keeps a very tight grasp upon the purse strings, and sits, as they say, firmly upon the old treasure chest; *Like a mountain, sat upon the plain.*

The mater, you will remember, is the Countess of Essex, and like all women with their own authority, she has a way with her. You know how mothers are when they get to a certain age, and you…well, you get to another, different age. And they seem strangely disappointed that you actually didn't die when that battleaxe nearly took your sword arm and the sabres rattled your brains, from one side of your head to the other as you spilled your precious life-blood, and watched it ooze, to be greedily swallowed by those dry, desert sands amid the slaughter, that was…Hattin.

I came out of the reverie as mother's voice rose in volume.

'…And why, Thomas Henry Valentine Devereux?' She threw the question at me.

'Why…have I paid all that good money? And to some heathen infidel? Ransom…do you think that I am made of money? Does money grow on trees? 'Cos if it do, then I wish I had an orchard or two…forsooth. Those heathen Germanic tribes have the right of it. They called it *'bad influence'* and they have it spot on.' She took a slight pause, purely for dramatic effect;

'Why, oh why, oh why…don't I introduce you to an heiress I know? A nice quiet girl…' she said pronouncing the word 'gal'.

'…she is a ward of court, and under the protection of a good friend of mine. Quite a pretty little thing really. And just of age. She is pious and modest, with a pure soul. And a very reasonable income too.

'She has a small castle, about a thousand acres,

with vine fields, and a mill, and the gift of a parish. And you know, the old provinces are really quite lovely still, if a little dilapidated by the constant attacks of the Routiers and the Free Companies. It really is time that you set aside this poor bastard girl of yours. Set her aside and settled down to life. Let's face it darling boy; there is nothing so sad as a bastard girl. It is so…unfortunate. At least a bastard boy can still rise high in this world.' She gave me a questioning look, which turned to a soft smile, as she sat next to me and took my hand. Then, more gently, yet still on the subject of my lover;

'Why, dearest son, why… oh why, do you insist on such an illicit affair? We have given you freedom to sow your oats. Have you not had your fill of this wench by now? She surely must be barren if you have not yet begat her with some bastard of your own. And a child…that *is* important. You must consider the succession!'

She stood and started to pace.

'Are you really so stupid? Stupid enough to think the king would give his permission for this union? That the Count, or even…that your father would agree?' She laughed.

'Not that his agreement is needed, but we should observe the proprieties.'

She crossed the room and picked up a stiletto dagger that lay on a chest. It was a new dagger - I had not seen it before. Even from where I sat I could see that it was a lethal weapon. It was made of well folded steel with an ebony handle that held a small glistened jewel, blood red, in the handle. It was made for throwing, as well as stabbing. It put me in mind of the attempt to assassinate The Marshall by Wat Sharpe. I wonder what ever had happen to Wat Sharpe. He is probably dead these five years or more. Then I wonder ed where the dagger had come from. It really was the last thing that mother needed, for each of her hairpins was just as lethal. Mother bounced the handle of the dagger up and down on her palm.

'And I won't start to mention that treasonous, traitorous, heretical family of hers.' She said, going on to mention them in quite some detail.

Of course I did not need the King's permission to marry, not being anywhere near the line of succession. Mother had needed permission but only as a formality, as she was descended from a Queen Mother, but what she meant, and what I had quite forgotten myself, was that the Lady Yvette, although a bastard, was still a ward of the court and descended from a distant royal line, and that *she* would need the King's permission to marry.

'…Look…Thomas, I know that it is difficult with your father. He never was an easy man, and well… let's face it, he does not think very highly of you… nor of me or your brothers, to be honest. Well except Robert…he can do no wrong! Still, I had hoped that…well, the princess…she is only a few moons older than you… and if you were to rejoin the Templars and be knighted…' I saw the smile light up her face.

'You know that your father has remove you from the line of primogeniture…but I will talk him around. Just give me the time. You will see. We old families; we must stick together, to survive, to prosper… and you, you *do* have your role to play but… you must set this girl aside. Really Thomas, don't you see? There actually is no other way. You need a good marriage, one that will re-establish your precedent…and in time, your father will come around. I know that I can talk him around.' She took my face in her hands and looked me straight in the eye. She was a powerful woman. Not young anymore, middle aged but still beautiful. There was no denying it. She stamped her foot and stomped off across the room again.

'Oh, how hopeless can you be. Do you understand the importance of such things?'

The mater had performed the above soliloquy yesterday morning, when I had been summoned to Deveroux House, a large half-timbered building, hard off The Strand, between the Temple and the river, and obviously, not far from the palace. And what is more, she performed it without taking a single pause for breath. She should be on the stage she would be an absolute sensation. I would speak to Marlowe about it. I'm sure he could write a part for her in one of his satirical performances. After all, Marlowe's friend Jonson had already written about my sister, Penelope, using her as his muse, Ocyte, in something called The Masque of Blackness. Whatever that was…

The upside of this soliloquy was that I hadn't had the opportunity to respond or, indeed, the need to give an excuse for not doing so. Mother had concluded by loosing her poison arrow and reminding me, in no uncertain terms, that she was the dominant force within the family;

' …And you had better remember it my boy. You are the fourth son. Remember, the fourth son.' She emphasised this with a vigorous shake of her finger;

'…and you are removed from the line of succession. We need to shake you out of this despondency. It's time you became a whole man again. You have done absolutely nothing since you returned from the crusades. Stop being such a lazy shit and sort yourself out!'

And it was true. For the last dozen moons I had been back at Pembroke College, Cambridge. Just fooling around with my artistic friends, living on handouts from my mother and the income from a few tasks that the mysterious Strix had handed to me.

'You've had enough study. Why not return to the Templars, finish your training and become a knight? If not, they need book-keepers too. And there is always the church. And…I know your Uncle Alexander, the Bishop of Ferns, a good man, is eager for your services. Your education may be useful after all. He needs a secretary, to help him with his histories of the conquest, and I'm sure you would enjoy the work. As I am sure you would enjoy Erin. I do hear that County Wexford is a beautiful, peaceful place. He often writes. Such long, meandering letters, but he is always firm on this.'

And picking up a parchment from the scribing table she went on to quote:

'… *A place that must have been built by the very gods themselves.*'

'Alexander writes that…' she said continuing;

'*The rivers are full of fish, which just seem to have nothing better to do than to leap out of the water and drop into the nets of their own accord…and there are golden fields, with orchards and beehives, and the hunting is quite excellent.*'

She peered at me over the top of the parchment.

'He goes on to say that; '*sometimes, it even stops raining for a whole hour or more…*'

Now that was a poison arrow or should I say three. The unfashionable, if not unmentionable, Catholic side of the family, the family involvement with the Templars, and Wexford, which really is buried deep within Erin's pleasant hills and vales. And, far, far, far away from my beloved metropolis, and even further away from my dear Yvette.

That, after all, was my mother's point.

3

The Banshee's Prophecy

Eveline, The Banshee of Craig Laith; *sits in the great elm tree and watches as Sir Richard De Clare, The Steward of the Forest of Essex, passes by, before making her way to Durty Nellies Inn, next to Bunratty Castle, in the Kingdom of Munster, Hibernia.*

It was early, not long after the fourth bell of the morning watch, and I sat in the mighty elm which stands near the ancient burial mound, hidden in the wild lands that surround Bunratty. My hooped stocking's legs dangling, swinging freely from the branch of my favourite tree. The morning mist hung heavy and I felt the moisture clinging to my face. I breathed in deeply and let my senses wonder for a while. Let nature flow into my mind, my body. And I felt her beauty, for this was Erin, the land of the gods.

The dream had been vivid. Stark - almost shocking in its brutal clarity. And I had a duty to perform. For that is the lot of the banshee. We are called on to deliver the messages from the Gods. The warning of the evil that is to come.

I watched the Norman coming into view. He was tall, with short red hair, which was shaved to the temples, as is their fashion. He was not a bad looking fellow. A suggestion of sadness floated briefly across my mind.

'For the Gods take a cruel delight in the misfortune of men.' I spoke softly to the magpie. She sat and watched with me. Oda was an old friend of my mother's and often paid me a visit when she was able.

The knight rode by. He surveyed the hills, the valleys and the bogs of the land. His army where encamped near by, at Bunratty Castle. I had watched them with interest as they arrived. Silly men fighting for a land they could never own. Who ruled here was irrelevant; for this is a land of high magic, and no mere human can ever rule over the magical beings. We let their world go by, like a shadow that passes with the sun, and we watched from the shadows, close enough to touch and yet invisible to their eyes. That is unless we wish to reveal ourselves.

And so Oda and I watched Sir Richard De Clare, The Steward of the Forest of Essex, as he rode through the mist. He studied the lay of the land, for even he knows that the morrow will bring the battle. His horse found the easier ways. He was a good horse, a Norman Trotter, sure footed and sturdy. Now he followed the sound of the running water, for the River Raite flows down by the castle, on its way to the Shannon and eventually he came to the clearing, where the mist and smoke fill the air, and here, next to the river, stands a pleasant old ramshackle inn.

Durty Nellies is famed far and wide as an hostelry. It has a reputation for its generous service and its meat and potato pies, and I often spend my leisure here, watching the people in their revels and listening to the energetic music. The king's new Cultural Laws are not enforced here. And even a young banshee needs a day off now and then.

Sir Richard dismounted and led the horse to the river. He patted the horse's neck as it bent to drink. Then he knelt down and I watched him from the

reeds as he removed his gauntlets and helmet, and
bent to drink.

'So the Norman will drink water…when Durty Nellies makes the best beer in a hundred leagues. This is
a strange one… eh'

Oda gave a small cry;

'pjur, pjur, weer…'

I waded into the river, upstream of the knight
and set about my task, folding the bloodstained
cloak deep in the water and began the washing. The
breastplate appeared amongst the reeds. Within only
a few moments the horse shivered, and pulled away
from the water's edge, omitting a frightful snort.
The waters had started to run red.

'Who are you washer woman?' asked Sir Richard.
I stood so he could seem me clearly. A young native
girl.

'In your language I am called Eveline. You could
never pronounce my true Gaelic name. It is far to
magical a name for your coarse tongue. I am the
Banshee of Crag Laith…The Holy Hill, where my sister Aine rules as Princess of the Fairies, and I rule as
Queen. We danced there that day… after Brian Boru
cleft your shields.' I told him.

I spoke softly but clearly, so that the message
would be easily understood. He looked shocked, and
I saw him check that his sword was loose. Yet he did
not draw it. He had no need and the river divided us.

'It is my task to wash the clothes of those who will
need them…when they journey to meet the Gods.'

'And who's blood is that upon your cloak?' the
knight asked.

'It's not my cloak. Do you not recognise your own
cloak? You know whose blood this is. Is this not your
crest upon the breastplate? It is your blood, Sir Richard. And the blood of your family! Go back to your
Frankish lands. You have no business here…none.

Only a cruel fate awaits you and your men on the morrow.'

And with this statement I waved my hands and let my body float away in the wind that blew amid the mists of Erin.

The warning had been delivered.

4

Morning Glory

Sir Thomas Devereux; *is in his rooms above the emporium of Messrs Camden and Sons, by royal warrant and appointment to his gracious majesty Edward II, Royal Astronomers, Astrologers, Cartographers, Chart Makers, Horologist, Navigators, Oikouménê, Scribists, and who are of the Worshipful Company of Painter-Stainers and Sporting Bookmakers, which are located in Neal's Yard, London. WC2H 9DP.*

I took another look at the seal and then threw the parchment on to the table and leaned back. I was in a pensive mood. The letter had disturbed my mind. I know it's not much of a mind…but at the moment it was greatly disturbed, I can tell you. Restlessly, I picked the parchment up again and resumed looking it over.

'Searching for a hidden meaning in a secret message?' I laughed to myself as I read it again.

My Dear Friend,

We are in danger and must remain ever vigilant. A message has arrived, it says:

'On this day, we have discovered, and had sight of a letter, that our friend

*Strix has intercepted; it is between
Dr John Dee and the Princess of the
bloode, Elisabeth.'*

*It is a strange document in truth,
my dear friend, I strongly urge you
to read it and right speedily too, for
it may be the key which unlocks our
struggle.*

*Go Here on the first Tuesday after the
moon is full.
N. D. IVB. DW.*

*But be careful I beg of thee. The walls
have ears, and sometimes they have
eyes too!*

*Remember ~ Black is the Badge of
Hell*

*Your fellow pupil, The Rakehell of
Canterbury*

'God's teeth.' I cursed under my breath.This, on top
of all other. What was going on? I turned the letter
over and inspected it again. It was a scrappy piece of
parchment, roughly edged and was obviously torn
hurriedly from some bigger manuscript.
'Cousin Bess?'
My mind raced as I thought of her. She had always
been so friendly towards me. And mother liked her

too. Was she in trouble? I inspected the letter again.

'This was worked in a hurry. That does not bode well. No, it is not good at all.'

However the seal was clearly displayed in the red wax, that was smeared across the back of the parchment and the code words had been used. I would have to risk it.

I heard light steps on the stairs and hurriedly folded and tucked the parchment safely within my robes. The door creaked as it started to open. Sir Anatole entered and looked at me. He stroked his whiskers slyly as he studied the room. His beady eye finally surveying a bread roll. He ignored my greeting. I started to explained to him my heartfelt predicament the fact that I was suffering from a lack of imagination and how this was affecting my writing; and that the publishers, Johanssons, were pressing me on the matter.

'A deadline, you know...' I let my voice trail off, as I slowly sipped at some wine and watched him.

'They will not give me a moment's peace. If I didn't need the money...I would soon give them short shrift. Speaking of money...do you have the rent? I'm afraid that Messr's Camden will be hoping for a payment.'

He really didn't seem to care about my troubles. Worse still, he didn't even take the time to pretend to care. I sometimes wonder why I let him stay with me at all. He contributed so very little to the household and though I often spoke to him, telling him all of my troubles, my problems, my plans, hopes and dreams. It was all for naught. I would even sketch out the odd storyline for him in order to gain his opinion of them, and sometimes, just generally shooting arrows at the clouds, as I've heard Marlowe call it. Yet it was all to no avail. As I say, he was a creature of a dark and sullen hue. And if we are going to get down to the nitty gritty, and the truth is being told, he was definitely not the best of companions. Most of the time, he didn't even take the trouble to acknowledge my very existence. Quite often he would laze about the place, sluggishly, laying on his back or his side, and chewing a mouthful of anything, and I do mean absolutely anything, that he could stuff in to his fat little cheeks, and all the while purposely ignore my every word.

Tonight, he sat lazily looking at my new stockings. They had fallen off my low bed, which was situated in the far corner of the room. I should mention that this was one of my favourite places. The bed I mean, not the far corner. Although to be fair, the far corner itself had nothing to feel ashamed about. No, the bed was definitely one of my favourite places in the whole, as my landlords Messr's Camden's maps had ably demonstrated, flat world.

The bed had arrived as a present from my cousin-uncle, Prince Louis, the Count. It was from the family seat at Everoux, in the Old Possessions of Gaul. And it was a truly magnificent bed. It had large, beautifully carved wooden scrolls that rose up from the legs like a colossus of old rising from the seas. They supported, and in turn were cushioned by, the heavy goose feather mattress and the deep furs and thick woollen blankets that emerged and gently kissed the duck feathered bolster.

With the exception of my allowance this bed currently represented my whole worldly wealth, and I loved nothing better than stoking up the fire, with a couple of big logs, and crawling into the old sleeping sack. I could stay there for days, pondering, sketching out storylines, deliberating, and philosophising and in fact I had. Four days was actually my current record for such an indulgence. And sometimes, if I was extremely lucky, I would not be alone.

Anyway, as I say, at this moment, Sir Anatole was over by the bed, and I strongly suspected that he was looking to steal my best stockings.

Lazily, I relocated my nightcap upon my head and scratched behind my ear. And then I stretched and manfully adjusted the crotch of my woollen leggings, having a vigorous scratch there too, as I re-folded the heavy, woollen robe and pulled the ends of the wide waist belt into an even tighter knot. I pointed through the window at the rain.

'We live in England; and the king would place a tax even upon the water.' I misquoted and muttering to myself, I slowly turned back towards the mess-strewn table which I used for all my literary works.

Sir Anatole stroked his dark brown whiskers and flicked a stunted little finger at a passing dust mote.

'I bet your king does not charge you a tax upon your water.' I said to him. As was usual he was in a grumpy mood. He gave me a look from his narrow, squinty, eyes, rolled up his mardy little face and pissed, long and manfully, managing to miss the pot but hitting the stockings with his aim, before storming off hurriedly to some quickly remembered engagement.

The latest tome, my masterpiece, was taking its own sweet time to unravel and I just knew that chapter twenty and three was going to be a pig, even before I had introduced the quill to the inkwell. Slowly, I bent to the fire and swung the hook that held the blackened kettle out and over the flames. Then I strode over to the wooden chest and removed an olive wood pestle and mortar and a small neat leather pouch. I held the pouch tightly and sniffed at it as I opened it, pouring out a handful of small, dark green and brown nut shaped pods. I dropped them into the mortar and started to break them up roughly. Each time I smashed the pestle down, I smiled with a grim satisfaction and crushed them in to small parts. And I could not help but think of my mother…my father…and bloody… Sir… bloody… Anatole…bloody…De Souris…bloody…Blanche. Down it went, hard and fast into the bowl, smashing, again, smashing, twisting, grinding, and I felt the pods, hard beneath the pestle, as they squashed with the sweetest, softest, cracking noise. I thought of the peasants in the shires and North of the Gap and wondered if their bones smelled so sweet, as they too were crushed, under the heavy pestle of the great empire and the royal crown.

My mind drifted to the Middle East where I had first found the beans. I could not help but re-membered my doomed crusade and Sir Rembald. I glanced at Red Feather and the memory of that sheering white heat washed over me. A sweltering heat. As the water and even the perspiration, from both man and beast, boiled away and the steam rose from Sir Rembald's armour. And the poor sad horses; dropping to their knees or just keeling over sideways as we rode. The blood boiled in their veins and their hearts burst within them.

The last I saw of the massive Templar he stood surrounded by heathens, helmet-less, his legs apart as he swung his mighty sword, Morena. He sheared through a spearman with one stroke, and with the return stroke, un-horsed a mounted man, taking half his arm in the swing. And then…well then I saw the infidel to my right and his sabre swinging towards my head. I tried to bring my shield across, to block the blow, but realised to late that it had been hacked to pieces, lost in the battle, hours ago and all that re-mained of it was a sliver of flimsy wood. The axe bit into my arm, and I felt a heavy blow to my head as something else hit me from behind. And I remember no more.

*Ride through the silent earthquake
lands,
Wide as a waste is wide,
Across these days, like deserts,
When pride,
And a little scratching pen,
Have dried,
And split the hearts of men,
Heart of the heroes, ride.*

Slowly there had come a distant, dreamlike memory of a man dressed in a white thawb. He was tending to my wounds. And later still, somehow, I was in Acre. And it was cool and peaceful…and soon, when I could walk again, I became aware that the stables were strangely silent; lost in their emptiness, as if the ghosts of our horses, now silent too, haunted them.

The relief party had found me amongst a pile of the dead. My arm was twisted and mangled and my leg and thigh had several arrows sticking out of them, like the feathers on a rooster.

And next came the fever.

Then a cool wind, the smell of the sea and the cracking, whip-like noise of the sails, and I was back in the gentle shade of the Mighty Constantinople. My arm was set and healing, the fever was a forgotten thing of the past, and my leg wounds just a distant memory.

Hattin was still a fearsome dream that haunted me in the night. John says that it is the true reason that I worked into the early mornings and beyond. He may be right.

Is it strange that no one ever asks me about Hattin?

Nor did anyone explain to me what exactly had happen to my knight, the Order, or the army of the King of Jerusalem. It is as if a dark shadow had fallen over the Templars. Surely, there must have been more survivors than the few that I had seen?

It was in Mighty Constantinople that I became seriously addicted to the beans. The habit had started to grow on me during my first visit to the High Gods guarded city, during the Ottoman campaign, and before we had sailed for Acre, and rode like conquerors into the holy city of Jerusalem. My fellow squires and I would make our way through the narrow streets, where the tall stone houses huggled lazily together and led down the hill from the vast castle keep to the small, smelly, and squalid district of the old city, next to the river market. An area called simply, *El Tahtakale.*

We would sit in the *Kiva Han* for hours, playing backgammon and chess, a pastime newly found amongst the Templars, and we would devour the dark distillation in small clear glasses, as we watch the stewards, sailors, merchants, fishwives, gypsies, tramps and thieves mingling in their own sweet mêlée.

Of course, back in the homeland, it is frowned upon to drink the dark liqueur. It is still seen as a filthy heathen occupation. Yet, in honesty, the beans are as easy to buy in London now, as opium is in Hong Kong. How else, other than war, but through trade in such commodities, could the Far East Company [incorporating India and Siam] and the Great Empire prosper? After all, a profit was always needed, so that the rich could get richer; and the poor… well they could die quietly. Lord Cecil, the Grand Chancellor is always searching for a new way to fill the treasury's coffers; and the King's taxes are always collected, even on contraband. Such is our world.

Soon, steam was rising above the kettle as it came to a rolling boil and I carefully emptied the contents of the mortars into a small wooden bowl, and folding my bell-shaped sleeve around the kettle's handle I poured the hot water over the crushed beans. An intense aroma permeated the room. I moved over to the cushioned window seat and waited for the sunrise to appear over the eastern docks, and hoped to see a Faerie Rainbow, as I sipped gently from the edge of the wooden bowl hoping not to burn my mouth.

'It is a new dawn and yet, sleep, o' gentle sleep… nature's soft nurse, thou hath alluded me?' I remember my friend Marlowe saying once. Then I re-read my opening chapter.

'Yes. That is better.'

I blew on the top of the bowl and gently leaned further back, sliding my fingers down and under the window seat. They found their targets, the little round notches which were embedded in the wooden tracery, secret and invisible to the eye. I moved the notch slightly to the left, activating the device and then I adjusted the volume level as the music began to play. Sipping the coffee, I stared out over Neal's Yard.

One glance through the window showed me all. The rain was slowing. In the braziers the last fingers of flame spat at the drops as they fell. The tapers above the doors had long been extinguished. And there in the sky the sweet forerunner of the goddess of dawn showed a dark grey smile, low in the morning sky.

And as I watched, I became intrigued by a small magpie, who was obviously a very early riser too. He darted from the shadow of a chimney to the eaves of the next building. He too sat there hunched up, observing, quietly watching the dawn, as the rain still slowly fell. We two listen, sharing the peace of the pre-dawn as Mr. Eddie '*Cleanhead*' Vinson's saxophone swirled as smoothly as ever and *Cherry Red* floated into the early morning air.

5

A Girl From The North Country

Sir Thomas Devereux; *is at the home of Lady Yvette Waterton, The Watermill, Axholme, which nestles in the bottom corner of Yorkshire, on the borders of Nottinghamshire and Lincolnshire, in that part of the Kingdom known as North of the Gap. DN10 6 HN*

You know those days when the sun is high at about the sixth bell of the morning watch and it never seems to want to fall in the sky?

Well no, to be honest, I'm not that familiar with them either. The fifth bell of the forenoon is far early enough for me. But, somehow, today I was up and about, dressed in my best doublet with scarlet hose and my knee length boots, and with only a stiletto dagger - my mother's actually, for ornamentation. It was tucked carefully into my broad leather waist-belt. And here I was; making my way through the small market town of Axholme.

It truly was a glorious day for the May Day celebrations and I was paying another visit to my sweet Yvette. Now, I don't know if you've ever been to the country or, for that matter, even to a small market town but if you haven't, here is, as they say in the tourist guides, the lowdown - Axholme is a busy little community, nestled in the bottom corner of Yorkshire, on the borders of Nottinghamshire and Lincolnshire; it has a royal charter for a market, another for an annual fair, and a third to operate as a small inland port. It was once, before the harrying, land belonging to Roger de Busli and earlier still a part of the Wapentake; That was when the Saxon and Vikingr roamed about the shop. It is North of the Gap. The surrounding area is forest. To the south stretches the great Sherwood Forest, to the north and west is the forest of Barnsdale. East, there are a few hills. Between the forest and the hills is mainly lowland marshes and wetlands, as the rivers Don, Trent, Idle, and their tributaries flood regularly, thus making a small inland sea. Yet these waterways are also the secret of Axholme's prosperity, and what makes it an inland port. Small ships and large boats are able to to navigate here from the wild northern seas. They progress along the Great Umber and into this small inland port and, from here, the rivers and canal networks can reach as far south as London, west to the industrial zone and to Liverpool, and even west by southwest to the Black Country, and further, as far as the great slave port of Bristol.

There was something else about the region too. And to be honest, though we rarely spoke of the matter, wounds still being fresh as it were, it had to do with Yvette's family.

Now, don't get me wrong, we were both from the highest of families - our families being of the *Companions of the Conqueror*. I am, of course, from the great house of Devereux, and my grandsire is Lord William, son of Richard, Count of Evereux, with his nephew, the head of our family, being none other than His Grace, Prince Louis of Evereux, and a half-brother to the King, Philip of France. We can trace our ancestry back to the First Vikingr, Rollo, and also to Richard The Fearless, ours and the Conqueror's great grandfather. Whilst my mother is of the Boleyn family, a daughter of a Queen Mother, and a true cousin of Her Grace, Bess Tudor, a Princess of the bloode.

Yvette's ancestry is more complicated, she being descended from the houses of Montbray and Monte Gomerie, and her grandsire being Geoffrey de Montbray, Bishop of Coutances, and one of King William's trusted prelates. As the story goes, she can trace her linage from the Vikingr King of Ringerike, Helgi *'The Sharpe'* Fridleifsson, on the one side, and Charlemagne and *Swanhild* on the other. Unfortunately Yvette had a problematic derivation, and her family had a rebellious nature. And let's face it, no king likes a rebel.

As I see it, the problem is that Axholme, which on the surface really does seem such a nice, quiet, idyllic kind of place is in reality, slap bang in the middle of a hot bed of insurgents, rebels, puritans, freethinkers and heretics. Particularly, but not limited to, the nearby villages of Scrooby, Misterton and Epworth; in which the Druids thrive and keep their faith alive through their off-spring heretics who between them give the crown such a hard time.

'And I must say…' I said, speaking to a small dog that had been walking along with me for a while,

'Even more importantly is the fact that this little town of yours is slap bang on Ermine Street and therefore has an easy journey by road, or indeed river and canal, back to the Metropolis.'

'Woof, woof!' answered the dog in agreement.

The other thing about Axholme is that the township is often confused with the mythical isle, and it's easy to understand why. As I said; the rivers Don, Trent, Idle and their tributaries, flood regularly and as the ground around Axholme is mainly marshlands, with a myriad of small lakes, which in turn are criss-crossed by deep streams and rivulets, the whole area becoming one huge inland sea. And some believed that there, in the midst of all this water, is a massive hill. The mystic Isle of Axholme. The fables and songs have it that the Isle floats around in the marshes and the mists of these border regions, and that it is the ancient home of the Druids. That may explain the host of freethinkers that seem to abound in the area and its environs.

Anyway, the people of the town had been about early today and there was a definite spirit of excitement in the air. I returned the smile that a beautiful young maiden had given me and I was very taken by the idea that, North of the Gap, some things still seem to be freer.

And so I strode down the high street, through the marketplace and there she was, standing with some people that I had not met, and she looked as radiant as a goddess; My Yvette.

Several pavilions were scattered about the village green - if a small market town can have a village green that is - and the local populace was bubbly and frisky as they mingled around the assorted stalls and tents. A small musical troupe played a rather noisy and slightly off-key tune with a huge amount of vigour, whilst the villagers and town folk cavorted around the beer stalls.

I must admit to being quite taken by all the fun and games, the colour of the whole thing but not at all tempted to join in. It all looked a little *too* much to me and I found the dunking stool, in particular, most frightful.

'The very idea of allowing all and sundry, for the price of a halfpenny, to hurl wooden balls at a iron plate just inches from your head is one thing, but to then consent to being dropped several feet into a tub of cold water, if they become successful in hitting the plate, is quite another.' I said to Yvette. Fortune, like the lady she is, had thankfully decreed that I would be spared these offences, as Yvette wanted to attend the church '*Sale of Goods*.'

Now, it occurs to me that Yvette was particularly fired up about this so called sale. Rather like a courser who, on seeing the hare, can't wait for the chap with the kerchief to wave the off. The resident priest was in full swing when we arrived, and blessing left, right, and centre, a host of varied goods and trinkets, which had been generously donated by the local merchants and their wives. He kept stressing that all should, and I quote, '*Dig deep* and *be not the last in coming forward*' as all the proceeds would go straight to the fund for the relief of the poor and towards the restoration of the church steeple which, like its cousin in nearby Chesterfield, is leaning at an angle which many find most alarming.

'You know, I'm not all together sure about these auction types of sales. I know that the Babylonians were very fond of them, and found it a good way to get hold of a new wife. However, it seems to me that neighbour *one*, gets rid of, or donates, as they say, several unwanted items, that another neighbour, call her neighbour *two*, has generously purchased or even I've heard say, received as an unwanted gift, from neighbour *three*, and given to the same, neighbour *one* that is. Only for neighbour *four*, to shell out the hard earned pennies to purchase them, at what seem to me to be a much-inflated price.

'I'm sure it would be far simpler for all concerned if neighbour *four*, was to wait her turn, so that neighbour *one*, can give the items to her, upon her birthday, or anniversary, or some other such occasion, and then simply make a gift of a few pence say, to the poor fund, or the steeple restoration fund, in church, at vespers of a Sunday.'

'You always were a wet blanket, Thomas.' Yvette replied when I mentioned this to her. And, of course, she is always right.

'The next lot is a pleasant box.' said the priest as we entered the pavilion.

'I call this the heathen lacquered box. Who will start the bidding? Who will offer me a thruppence for this beautiful inlaid wooden box?' said the priest hopefully.

'No. Two pennies? Ah, thank you Captain Gordon,' he continued and nodded over to one of the rosy cheeked, weatherbeaten, brusque type of chaps.

'Any bids on tuppence?'

'Three!' shouted out my dear Yvette.

'Three and a half,' said a large gent with even rosier cheeks, who stood near the entrance to the pavilion.

'Three and a half - now come on My Lords, Ladies and Gentlemen, this really is a most unusual collection, who will give me four? Ah, thank you sir, do I hear five?'

'Five pence!' stumped up Yvette.

'Six.' interjected the large gent with the rosier cheeks.

'Thank you. That is a silver sixpence from Captain Gordon, oh excellent, most generous. Do I dare ask for seven?'

Yvette raises her arm and shouts out 'Seven pennies!'

'Seven pennies, to Lady Waterton, any more bids?' asks the priest as he looks around the tent. The crowd looked around with him, as seven pennies was one of the higher bids of the afternoon.

And, as they look around, their eyes travel instinctively to Captain Gordon, who shakes his head, admitting defeat. All eyes now fell on the large gent with the rosier cheeks, who was still standing at the rear. The colour of his left cheek spread and blended perfectly with that of the right cheek, forming a mask of scarlet right across his face, and he shuffled his leather booted feet in a very awkward manner. His face took on the aspects of the world map, where the empire is highlighted in pink.

He reminded me so much of a dear school colleague, old Pug Mosham - the finest inebriate that ever staggered down Wardour Street.

He is dead now of course. It was that new fad for drinking the leaves of the tea that did for him.

Poor old Pug - he became so found of the brew that he was even known to refuse wine or beers. One day, as he was walking through London, a whole bale of the stuff fell from a hoist and broke his neck. Dead. Just like that.

And it just goes to show that no good can come from forsaking wines and beers for the evil that is tea.

Anyway, the chap who reminded me of old Pug lifted his eyes up to see my dear Yvette staring at him with what some people would call a very hard stare.

Under that stare what little courage he had managed to muster deserted him by the cargo load, and he shuffled his feet again.

'No further bids?' said the priest rather despondently.

'Very well. Going at seven pence, twice at seven pence, sold at seven pence to Lady Waterton.'

'Oh, how wonderful - don't you just love a bargain Thomas?' said Yvette,

'Now then, let's have a look at the refreshment tent.'

As it happens, I really have a very cavalier attitude towards the sale of goods, especially the country sale. I can take them or leave them, so to speak, but I thought I had better keep shtum about the subject.

'That's more like it.' I said: 'Refreshments.'

'I bet it is a tent full of warm beer and cold women though,' I thought to myself.

And it was.

6

The Bloode Moon

Sir Thomas Devereux; *is at the home of Lady Yvette Wa-terton, The Watermill, Axholme, which nestles in the bottom corner of Yorkshire, on the borders of Notting-hamshire and Lincolnshire, in that part of the Kingdom known as North of the Gap. DN10 6 HN*

It was a still, starlit night and Yvette and I walked along the river bank. The Idle flowed slowly along its merry path; while Perseus and Andromeda ran, jumped, and bounced as they pranced in the long grass of the meadow.

'They will need bathing before we let them in the house,' Yvette declared. I agreed and pulled her close to steal a kiss.

'And me too?' I asked her.

'Of course…yet we will never get that mind of yours truly clean.'

The moon was full and bright, and a gentle breeze wafted down from Windmill Hill and across the water meadow. As the moon passed behind a small cloud, a very strange thing happened.

The hounds in the kennels started to howl and Perseus and Andromeda stopped stock still and joined them. The moon re-emerged from behind the cloud, the first slim crescent of it becoming visible, and a strange phenomenon took place. The upper horn of the crescent split in two. From the mid-point

of the division, a flaming torch seemed to spring.
It spewed out over a considerable distance; a shot
of fire, hot coals and sparks. The body of the moon
which was below, seemed to writhe like a wounded
snake. This happened a dozen times or more, and as
the moon emerged fully, it took on a dark hue. The
whole round moon shone a deep, dark, red. A Bloode
Moon.

'Holy Avenging Angels! The Gods must be angered
by something!' I exclaimed.

'It is the bloode moon Thom! Not something I
thought I would ever see. Something evil is afoot...'

'You have heard of this before?' I asked her.

'I...' She paused and looked away, before returning
her gaze to me. Her eyes held mine for a few moments longer than normal. Then she spoke again.

'It is the work of the three ancients of the craft.
Luna, Phoebe and Selene. It has long been prophe-
sied that the Bloode Moon will appear. It is a portent.
It tells us that evil is abroad. And now...they have
stepped out of antiquity. Men should look to their
loved ones this night...'

She shivered as she pulled her shawl close and bent
to settle the dogs. I stroked Andromeda's neck and
continued to stare at that dark red moon for a few
more moments before I turned to follow her back to
the mill. The night had grown decidedly chilly.

7

And So It Begins

Doctor John Dee; stands at the window of his solar and looks out over the orchard garden which slopes down to the river. River House stands in large grounds, between the High Street and the river Thames, next to the church of St Mary the Virgin, in Mortlake, London, SW14 8JA.

I stood back from the window and pulled at my beard. It was long and white, and my soul felt the same. I was in a pensive mood. Slowly I replaced the leather caps over the ends of my spy glass. The Bloode Moon shone down on me; as if the Gods held a torchlight high above above my head. And I don't mind telling you that I was disturbed.

There was a soft knock on the door of my solar and my wife Jane entered in her demure fashion. She bent her head towards me, as if apologising for interrupting my work, and announced;

'John, there is a messenger for you. He is from the Countess of Essex.'

'Eh? A Message? For me? From Lettice Knollys? What could that damned woman want at this time of night?'

Jane moved across the room and handed the small folded parchment to me and lay a hand on my chest. Her eyes danced with amusement and her smile was soft and knowing.

'Don't work all night dear,' she said as she moved

back to the door.

'The runner is waiting in the kitchen for a reply,' she said quickly with a nod of her head as she left the room pulling the door tight behind her.

I noticed The Knollys' seal in the deep red wax. It lay adjacent to that of the Countess of Essex. I broke them both with a quick snap and began to read;

Doctor Dee,

Forgive me contacting you like this;
I have urgent need of my son Thomas.
I know he is with that witch.
Yet I have not the time to instigate a search.
It is possible that you know his whereabouts.
His brothers, Walter and Francis are dead.
It is imperative that he returns to Essex
House immediately.
Please use you skills to contact him directly.
I will, indeed, be indebted to you,

Lettice Knollys
Countess of Essex.

'And so it begins...'

8

Trial By Water.

The Witchfinder General; and his trusty lieutenant, John Stearne, have gathered a large crowd who watch eagerly as they conduct their investigation of the two local witches. They are gathered at the village green, next to the Duck and Hound, Hatfield Perverel, in the County of Essex. CM3 2JF

In a nearby oak tree, four pairs of eyes watch the scene with trepidation. One pair are bright green, another a dazzling blue. The last, the darkest of blacks, are very far away.

The young woman was tied by her hands and feet, sturdily secured to the old wooden chair. She swung in the air. The Ducking Stool, as it is called, was submerged for the second time.

'Tell me Mistress Waterhouse…will you now confess your sins or will you have Sterne here prick your skin? Confess…for it is certain that the devil will not confess for you.' I said.

I spoke loudly, so that all the village could hear, for it was important to my work that we adhere to the rituals of a trial. A confession was of the essence. It was needed for a conviction. The Innkeeper stood next to me, proud and erect. He was an arrogant man. He relished his association with Stearne and myself.

The girl had not answered. I had not expected her to for she was now a foot or more under the water.

Her dark blonde hair floated wildly about her head. We kept the stool submerged, all eyes studying the swirling mass of hair. The confession would come later. Later; when we had her in private; naked, and at our complete mercy. A small smile spread across my face and I felt a stirring.

A black cat hissed at my man. Stearne heaved a stone at it. He was too slow. The cat had swaggered away.

'See how even her familiar deserts her now? Such is the power of our gods!' Shouted Stearne. The crowd roared their enthusiasm. I nodded my approval and then indicated for the ducking stool to be swung upward again.

The men of the village grinned excitedly as the half naked maiden was slowly raised from the water. She bounced violently in the air as the arm of the stool reached its apex, for the men had been zealous in their labours. Water streamed from her torn and tattered gown and it clung to her nubile figure, revealing her form for all to see.

Her hair was matted to her head and she spluttered as she coughed the water from her lungs. She stared madly at the crowd, searching, seeking any salvation. There was none.

Still, it was plain to see that the villages did not truly wish her any particular harm. They were scared. And they kept their tongues silent, for if she was to be acquitted, then…who next would be accused?

The Innkeeper glared at the crowd. His men held the older witch tight. Some said the crone's home-brew was too good for him to compete with. He was the one who had proffered the charge, and he had paid my fee. He had hired a man of zeal. For it was my mission to hunt out a witch in every village. I had a calling...one that paid well.

✪

The last pair of watching eyes were indeed far away. A two-day ride or more. They watched through the eyes of the others three, the images floating through the crystal, split like light through a prism. These eyes had a voice, and it whispered to the other watchers;
'Now!' they heard the voice say softly in their minds.

✪

Suddenly a storm of black and white feathers flew close to the crowd, and the elder of the two witches broke free. Several of the men, who had held her, cried out aloud and began patting furiously at their garments, which had suddenly begun to smoulder.
'Exsecratus sum in gehennam te.' the voice screamed at me.
'I curse you Witch Finder...and your evil deeds... curse you...until the ninth generation!'
Unseen and very far away a thumb flicked from behind teeth and threw the gesture at the Witcher with long soft fingers.
'I am the only witch here. Let the girl and crone go.' said the voice.
'Iron you fools...you must hold a witch with iron chains.' I cried at them. My midnight black mare danced in a circle, scared by the incorporeal voice.
'John, get her held fast! For now she has confessed...'

'Riik-rak-rak-rak. Wock, wock, wock a wock!' the magpie cried as a cloud passed over the noonday sun. And with a simple swirl of a distant, unseen hand, the Crone Witch of Hatfield Perverel faded from view, like a mist dissolving in the morning sun. A loud gasp ran through the crowd, and they turned to run for their homes. And just as quickly, they too had had disappeared.

From a shadow I saw a pair of bright green eyes flash hatred at me. I looked again.

Gone, within a moment.

I sought to take my anger out on the girl but she too was gone. Her ropes were cut and floated freely on the surface of the pond.

'Find her!' I screamed.

✪

The two witches sat on my kitchen floor rubbing their sore bottoms. I had not been given time for a soft landing. The older witch held her granddaughter tightly. She looked around in amazement. The young girl sat shivering, she sobbed. A large puddle spread around her on the stone floor.

'Welcome,' I said. It was a voice that had only a few moments before been inside their heads.

'Here take this towel and dry yourself. There are dry clothes in the bedroom. We are of a size. Maybe you're a bit thinner...' I sniffed.

'Will you take tea or maybe something stronger?' I asked the Grandma.

'I have a fine French brandy.' I said as I walked across to the dresser.

'This is Yorick. He is my...companion.'

Yorick sat in the corner working on a chess problem. He looked quite at home. He had his hat on, and he wore a long dark cloak. At one side of his chair lay several open books.

He stood, removed his pipe and hat, before he took a bow. Just as if it were normal that a skeleton should live in the corner of your kitchen.

'The others will be here…' I was interrupted by a popping sound, as a cat and a magpie landed on the kitchen table. The cat licked his whiskers and swaggered away to look for something to eat.

'Wock, wock, wock a wock, pjur, pjur…,' said Oda, telling the tale, as she flew, to land on Yorick's naked skull.

The old lady gapped at the scene. The young girl sobbed some more and shyly covered herself with the warm towel. As she did, a tall dark shadow fell across the the open kitchen door. A small urchin appeared on the threshold.

'Here's Nosher!'

9

The Smell of War

***Sir Thomas Devereux;** is secluded with his lover, Lady Yvette Waterton, in her home at The Watermill, in the small market town of Axholme which nestles in the bottom corner of Yorkshire, on the boarders of Nottinghamshire, and Lincolnshire, in that part of the Kingdom known as North of the Gap. DN10 6HN*

A miasmatic stench hung over the land, spreading like a malevolent plague, pervading each and every individual, and everywhere the word was whispered…WAR.

Far away, in the arms of my sweet Yvette, I slumbered. Snug-a-bed, peaceful and beatific. I woke slowly as a beam of sunlight strolled across my face and, raising my head, I selected a morsel and began nibbling at a breakfast of bread and soft cheese.

We lay in each others arms, sweet and quiet. We watched the world go by. Soft clouds floated in a clear blue sky, and dragonflies danced with the dust motes as they floated in the rays of the golden sun. Peace drifted over the millpond and through our bedroom window. It settled over us.

For nearly a week now I had been lazing around, thinking, mulling, pondering, or just walking in the woods and meadows. Time, like the river itself, stood still. The river wove its way past the mill and meandered out to the wild northern seas.

The Idle - a good name for a slow river.

The world held a bliss of its own and life was tranquil. The horrors of Hattin were beginning to fade from my mind, as Yvette's love brought a solace to my soul. I am sure she had weaved a calming spell upon me.

I lay back and fed a piece of cheese to Oda, Yvette's strange magpie, who cocked her tail and hopped from the bedpost to the clothes chest. Oda was a peculiar, mysterious, and somewhat sinister bird.

She had deep blue slashes on her body, and terrible dark eyes which showed absolutely no light in them. Still, Yvette loved her.

I have absolutely no idea why.

And so it was, in my languid bliss, that I consequently knew nothing of the conditions of the realm. Not a thing outside of my own myopic vision. And a vision she was to mine own eyes. She was tallish, about the same height as me, and she had curves and bumps in all the right places. Her hair was as golden as the new churned butter, and it hung down to her waist. It draped across the perfect summer peach of her buttocks.

She had dazzling, sapphire-like eyes, dark lashes and eyebrows that arched teasingly. Perfectly pouty lips of a cherry red. All this, and an educated mind, that could hold even Dr Dee at an arm's length. Our love had reached its fifth year, and it seemed to me, on this bright, late summer's morning, as though it would spread through the future, smooth and endless...forever.

But now, temporarily at least, I was needed elsewhere.

The summons had been delivered by what I can only describe as a collection of dirt and hair, with an aroma of horse, wet dog, and dung. I was unable to comprehend what this urchin was saying - if indeed it was an urchin. All I know for sure is that, in the metropolis, that is what it would have been called. But here in rural Axholme…well you could never be sure. I was also unsure about was the urchin's gender; in all honesty, it could have been anything.

'It seems that I am summoned. Two messages in one day.'

'Oh Thom, when do you have to leave?' She looked annoyed.

'It's not your mother is it - how did she find you?' She looked frightened.

'Two Messages?'

'Not mother, no. Well not directly.' I reassured her.

'One *is* from mother via Doctor Dee, and the other is from Strix. And between them they can find anybody.'

I took her in my arms, and she came willingly, knowing that I had to leave. And so, later that day, I was mounted on my roan mare, travelling back to the metropolis and as Strawberry and I strode south, the whole world began to hum.

Softly at first. Like a bee on a summer's afternoon, that drifts past your window on the day's soft breeze. Then more insistently, like a mosquito in your bedchamber, after the candle has been extinguished.

Here was whispered a word from a fellow traveller. Then, a warning from a merchant at the inn. And as the buzz built, somehow a feeling deep within me, that I too had to return with more haste, began to build;

A word;
'The queen had been feathered on the orders of Badlesmere's wife.'

A whisper;
'*The queen was dead.*'

A warning;
'*The southern nobles have risen again.*'

A cry;
'*War was upon us all.*'

Then, it was a swarm of angry hornets.

A moan;
'*It's Lincoln, all over again!*'

A Shout;
'*The barons and the king were at each other's throats again. But it was the women, who had started it all.*'

And in truth, it was all of the above, and none of them at all.

For war is not new to the people of the Great Empire. In fact, we are at war constantly. It is the normal way of life for the nobles and their entourages. We were born to war, we were trained for war, we fought in war and we made our living from war. War was our raison d'être.

At school we had learnt from Dr Mirabilis, that: '*The whole economic, religious and social structure of the Great Empire is built upon constant expansion, exploitation, booty, theft, and manipulation of the subjugated, resultant in enforced commerce and taxes.*'

And of course, that meant perpetual war.

And really, we knew nothing else. The empire has its wars everywhere, and has done for as long as anyone could remember. I learnt at Cambridge that the wars had been waged for over eight hundred years.

Although the great Dr Dee believed that: *'Time is irreverent, just a bright gleam in the eye of the beholder.'*

Still it really was a different thing for the people of the land. They knew about the wars.

They profited from the wars, for they made goods and sold their harvest to the Empire. Some even went off to fight in the wars. And some came back. And if they did, they were made men. They had become men of substance and wealth. However, the small people, the common man, did not usually experience anything of the wars themselves, not at first hand; and this was different. This was a war within the kingdom.

It was at the Templars', an inn in their own town of Bladock, that I heard news;

A Roar;
'They have murdered our Boys; At Rouen, they have murdered our boys.'

I exited hurriedly. Still, I could not fail to notice the red hazel tree that stood in garden of the Templars' Inn. I had fastened Strawberry to a rail that stood close by. The trees leaves were still dripping from the recent rain. The drops falling into a pool at the tree's trunk. A deep crimson pigment spread through the small pool. It shone a blood red. The stain spread quickly, like death. An omen. It was then that I kicked Strawberry into a furious pace.

10

Murder At The Castle

The Tears of Hermes introduce Our Special Correspondent;
William Camden.

A Report of the action at The Siege of Rouen, in the Old Possessions of Gaul.

***The Noble Brothers Devereux
Murdered
by Franks
Siege of Rouen.***

Terrible news here from the Siege of Rouen, in Old Gaul, where Sir Robert Devereux [25] and his troops fight nobly for the King. The aim - to recapture the city from the evil Franks.

On May Day, in the great village-town called Pavillie, nearby the city of Rouen, there was a mighty skirmish, where our brave troops led by Sir Robert's brother Francis Devereux [21] were trapped in crossfire by one Alain Blanchard [30] and his crossbow men. A devilish weapon that is forbidden in war by none less than the Pope himself.

Badly injured Francis Devereux fell from his horse. His brother Walter Devereux [23], known to all as 'A diamond of our time', led a heroic charge and recovered his injured brother and most of the trapped men, before he, himself, was overrun by the Frankish forces. The brothers Devereux and six others were capture and secured within the city walls.
And that night, Sir Robert himself fell upon the town of Pavillie and did bring it to fire. In less than an hour it was all burnt to the ground, so that the Frankish had much ado and did lose many troops and carriages.

Upon learning the identity of his prisoners and their relationship to Sir Robert, the Frankish leader, this Alain Blanchard, defied all the laws of chivalry. The next morning with a great show and performance, and in front of the castle; the whole army, all eight noble men, including Sir Walter and the badly injured young Francis Devereux, were taken at the point of a sword and hanged from the walls of the city.

Credit; William Camden, Special Correspondent, The Castle of Rouen,

Old Gaul.

'Our correspondent, William Camden, was truly appalled by this flagrant breach of the 'Code of War' and we, the editorial staff of the 'The Tears of Hermes' demand, on your behalf, that The King should instigate reciprocal action immediately. We demand their Revenge.'

~ The Editor. ~

11

Blind Bartimaeus

Sir Thomas Devereux; *is in his rooms above the emporium of Messrs Camden and Sons, by royal warrant and appointment to his gracious majesty Edward II, Royal Astronomers, Astrologers, Cartographers, Chart Makers, Horologist, Navigators, Oikouménê, Scribists, and who are of The Worshipful Company of Painter-Stainers and Sporting Bookmakers, which are located in Neal's Yard, London, WC2H 9DP.*

As you can imagine, yesterday's reunion at Devereux House, was not a happy one. It had been an emotional meeting.

Mother was distraught. She was badly hurt. I don't believe that I have ever seen her in such a state of composure. The Lady Margret, the wife of my brother Walter was also present. Poor Margret was truly hysterical. They had been married less than a year. For her to lose her husband and we, as a family, to lose two sons…it was indeed shocking news. I couldn't help but think that Father would be annoyed.

The special correspondent for *The Tears of Hermes* was none other than my landlord's son William. Samson Camden's son that is, not Manoah's son, who is called Jedediah, if that is possible.

We had been at Winchester together. William and Jedediah and I. Not for long, obviously, as they soon asked me if I would not be happier at Kings'. William had also been a student of John Dee's and was probably working for Dee, Strix and Walsingham in this spying club of theirs. Which I am afraid that I can't tell you about because, as everyone knows, it's a secret organisation.

Anyway William had written a very nice letter to Mother informing her of the sad news before it appeared in '*The Tears*', which I thought was very considerate of him and I made a special point of praising him for that to his father, when I returned to Neal's Yard. He had apparently written to his father too. Probably suggesting that all outstanding rent be collected quickly.

Quite a boy our William…

And so it was with a heavy heart that I pottered around the next morning. I had a meeting with Strix later but for now I needed coffee. I leaned out of the window and whistled at the old man as he shuffled through Neal's Yard. His dog tagged along behind him, belching and farting noisily. They are both a common sight in the neighbourhood, and quite a remarkable source of information, when sober, for they are both complete inebriates. They pass this way most every afternoon, on or around the bell of the First Dog Watch.

The old man's name is Bartimaeus but everyone calls him Blind Bart. The dog he calls Black Spot, who as it happens, is neither black nor spotted. Immediately Bart's head swung around and those hollow eyes of his looked up at me. The king had put his eyes out nearly half a decade ago. His crime? Distributing seditious pamphlets, with the intent to forment revolution. Some say he was among the architects of the revolts and dissent that are now spread through the kingdom, particularly North of the Gap. It is suggested that only his age, and the good King's kind heart, saved him from being hung, drawn, and quartered. Others suggested that he was spared only to serve as a constant reminder to those who would harbour seditious thoughts. Still, a third opinion is that he turned his coat and became an informer. I remember that John Dee had told me that Bart's daughter is lodged at Scarborough Castle; a guest of the king.

Blind Bart had languished in the White Tower for a number of years and then, to celebrate the Feast of St Lucia, and kick off the Christmas holidays with a bang, the King had him brought before the court, when they had finished their dining, and the poor man was ceremonially blinded with a red hot iron. A poker that had two tines, measured perfectly to bridge the nose.

'Yes… Sir Thomas, *The Tears*…Sire?' he asked as he held forth today's copy of The Tears of Hermes. The daily newssheet that was published by my friend, Johansson the publisher.

'Terrible news we has of your brothers Sire, and more…now the latest news of your father's campaign in Tara. The battle of Dysert O'Dea…more tragic news, Sire…tragic. We are all damned…of that I'm sure.'

He smiled a crooked smile. I tossed him the halfpenny and watched as he threw the paper up to me. It hit the wall below my window, and a good deal to the left.

'Well caught Sire.' Bart said, with out the slightest trace of sarcasm and, smiling, he lurched off across the yard with a simple wave of his hand. Black Spot belched, struggled to his feet and, staggering only momentarily, followed his master, his stride rhythmically punctuated by the sound of breaking wind.

12

Owain The Red Hand

Strix is located in the small front bar of The Magpie Inn, which is situated in that maze of depravity, known locally as Grub Street, London. EC2Y 9DP

It is not often that I head north of the city wall, not by foot anyway. I truly dislike walking about London. It is so…smelly. And yet the messenger had been most insistent.

Lorenzo had been a small magpie, and one who I had not met before. He had arrived at Tweezer Alley early in the morning. That, in itself, was a surprise. I keep my location more secret than I keep my secrets. Still, a magpie does have a knowledge that others do not possess.

His message was simple;

'Riik-rak-rak-rak. Wock, wock, wock a wock. Pjur, pjur, weer, weer. Queg, queg, queg.'

He had said no more. He had not had the opportunity. Petrosinella sprang, and devoured him with relish. A mango chutney I believe. Right there on the hearth rug.

'That is really is no way to treat a guest!' I scolded her.

Now, I don't know if you have ever tried to scold a cat yourself…but the result is that they react with what I have heard described as extreme prejudice. Petrosinella had zoomed away; out through the window. In the manner which I can only describe as… well, a scalded cat. She crossed the roofs of Temple Bar, and hid behind the crooked chimney of an adjacent building. From here she looked at me with an almighty disdain. She really is becoming a handful. And I am still not sure about her loyalty at all.

Her showing up when she did always seems just… too opportune. I often speculated about her being a foreign agent. Perhaps in the service of either Frankia or España. Maybe, Gods forbid, even Anjou.

Petrosinella had moved in a few years ago. Then, she had been a grand old lady with long grey hair and bright green eyes, and she had the most pleasing aspect and demeanour. And now, somehow, she seemed to be getting younger, thinner, taller, and definitely more crotchety. She was unquestionably becoming more…gingery. The grey was fading from her hair, and a bright streak of ginger had appeared. It was slowly spreading along her back from her head to her long luxurious tail. And her nature is definitely becoming, what I have heard Dr John Dee elucidate in his scholarly manner, as tetchy, testy, waspish, prickly, peppery, touchy, irritable, irascible, crusty, and defiantly cantankerous.

'I know someone who is going to be mightily vexed about all this. Don't you know that we do not kill the messenger? It's written in the Code of War. Did they teach you nothing at school?'

I shouted at her through the open window, as I swept the remains of Lorenzo onto the coal shovel, and threw them out of the opposite window where they narrowly missed a passerby and collided with the post box, before eventually landing in a heap amongst the mud and mire of Water Street. They would not be there long. The local rats, cats, dogs and children would see to that.

And so here I was, exiting through the Cripplegate, where the guards threw me their menacing looks, and crossing Fore Street before entering the labyrinthine network of small alleys and courtyards that interweave and spread northwards. Some said that you could walk east to west, and north to south, across the whole mile of Grub Street, without a ray of sunlight ever falling upon your shoulder. It was not something I had the inclination to try. As I approached The Rams Head, I could see The Seven Stars, which lay next to The Red Lyon, just off Lyons Inn Court, where people like Oliver Cromwell and John Dee were often to be found, spreading their revolutionary zeal like butter upon newly toasted bread.

The Kings Arms, The George Inn, The Greyhound Inn, The King's Head, and The Blue Boar, are all huddled into that small crammed space on the edge of Gun Alley, which itself runs across Grub Street, just where The Peacock meets The Red Bull, next to The Bell, and across from The Three Legs. Here too The Sugarloaf, The Flying Horse, and The Half Moon all stand and watch as the world strides past, as does The Bull and Bell, The Man in the Moon, The Crown, The Swan, and The Red Rose. I made my way around the corner, always heading east and carefully keeping my face concealed within my hood. I passed Lloyd's Brewhouse, The Horse Shoe, The Three Herrings, The Black Raven, and The Three Tuns, before I found the Magpie Inn.

The inn's sign showed a beautiful magpie, regally sat upon a branch - on her head was a golden crown. I shuddered slightly at the memory of the dead messenger, and wondered if this was a precognitive vision; and I knew that the messenger's death would have to be answered for. Like dark storm clouds, trouble loomed on the distant horizon.

I immediately recognised Kit Marlowe as I entered the small front bar. He sat at a small table in the corner, with his back to the wall. I glanced at him swiftly and manoeuvred myself onto the same bench, so that I sat adjacent to him. A man, who some called Honest John, passed the table. He hands out pamphlets of *The Sentinel* to all who would take them. As he passed he stroked his finger down the length of his nose. Marlowe returned the signal. Not a word was said.

Keeping my hood on I slid along the bench a little, so that our heads were as close together as those of strangers could be. The serving woman, sometimes called Maggie, approached the table and gestured at me, proffering her wares. I nodded, and placed a halfpenny upon the table. She smiled a gap toothed smile, showing a scattering of gold, a sign of better times maybe, before placing a tumbler in front of me and filling it with a dark brown beer.

'I have news from the court. Happenings in the west country. It may be of great import. It may be nothing but gossip.' Marlowe said as he raised his glass. His voice was swallowed by the general cacophony of the room.

'It concerns Margret, Baroness Badlesmere and Her Grace.' He slurped at his beer before continuing.

'On her way from Caerleon to Oxford, Margret was taken captive by a band of Welshmen, led by Owain the Red Hand, a small lord of the Welsh Marches. He claims to be the true Prince of Gwynedd, and of Wales.' He wiped his hand over his mouth.

'The leader of the notorious Free Company? Owain ap Thomas ap Rhodri? His band of welshmen fought for Frankia at Poitiers. I did not know he was back in England,' I said to my sleeve.

'And he is the rumoured to be the lover of The Queen's sister, Catherine de Valois,' he continued to a fly that passed.

'This is a dangerous liaison. And the Queen's association with him is…well, disloyal at the very least.'

I studied a painting of a haywain that had broken down at a river crossing. The repair men were trying to change the wheel. The insignia of their guild clearly visible on their smocks - Royal Carriage Alliance.

It was then that a small man, who was dressed in black velvet and wore a large felt hat of the same colour, sat close by us. He ran his fingers around his huge lace collar in a nervous manner, and looked thoughtful as he and Marlowe started to converse for a while. The small man removed his hat, revealing a large dome-like bald head, which had a few strands of hair stretching their length over the top of the dome, and that seemed to be held in place by what I believe was goose grease.

He listen earnestly to all that Marlowe had to say to him, nodding his head vigorously, and all the while stroking small his goatee beard. Their talk was all about literature and the theatre.

I studied the room. The place was full of literati, and pamphlets and newssheets were circulating from table to table, each incurring excited comments as they did. In a corner, I thought I recognised a man I knew from Bethnal Green…yet I could not place his name. He saw me watching him, and looking uneasy, he scuttled from the room, as if to make for the jakes.

'What was his name?' I thought. Then Marlowe broke my reverie.

'And this Welshman demanded a ransom, as is usual in such circumstances. A hundred shillings for her release. She was held prisoner for one night. They say that she was brutally raped by this Owen, who they also say, used her abhorrently in all truth. However, the story which has been spread around the court is that it was all twenty of the Welshmen that had her; and that she was a most willing participant too.' Marlowe drank deeply.

'Hugh De Spencer, the younger - he is nephew to the Merchant Marcus, who has his emporium in Oxford Street - arranged for her release. He himself is betrothed to Joan of Arce, the King's sister,' Marlowe said, resuming his tale, and still without glancing once in my direction.

'The brigands were arrested and held in Cardiff. And yet within ten days they were released, and without a charge or penalty, save for a hundred shilling to Lord Badlesmere, for trespass upon his property.' Marlowe gave a salutation to a passerby before continuing;

'Her grace was heard to comment to her ladies-in-waiting that '*Such a poor meretrix, has done very well to earn five shillings a head.*'

'God's teeth! This is the woman's work. I have no doubt. That it should come to this... Still I cannot rule out that His Grace was aware of this situation or that he may have been instrumental in its implementation.'

I finished my drink.

'I can say no more on that subject, you understand?' I concluded as I rose and made my way out into the maze that is Grub Street.

13

The Tears of Hermes

Sir Thomas Devereux; is in his rooms above the emporium of Messrs Camden and Sons, by royal warrant and appointment to his gracious majesty Edward II, Royal Astronomers, Astrologers, Cartographers, Chart Makers, Horologist, Navigators, Oikouménê, Scribists, and who are of The Worshipful Company of Painter-Stainers and Sporting Bookmakers, which are located in Neal's Yard, London, WC2H 9DP.

Once the news sheet had been retrieved, I poured some more coffee for myself and took up a comfortable position on the widow seat. It was several bells before my meeting with Strix at the Nellie Dean. On the wax cylinder Mr Eddie 'Cleanhead' Vinson was retelling a story from the Colonies incorporated in his song *'Juice Head Baby,'* and once again he was complaining about his sodden lover. I listened intently while I perused the sporting news at the back of the paper first, and my heart lifted as I read the report of The Wednesday beating Sir Henry 'Harry Hotspur's' Percy's team, usually called *'The Spurs,'* by a score of twenty and five to ten and four. There had been only seven fatalities. I remembered those school days. Yvette and I had been at the King's school in Lincoln with Hotspur and we had become firm friends. Another friend that I had not seen for a while. Still… he too was in Old Gaul now, with my brothers…brother…I corrected myself and glanced at my damaged sword arm and cursed a little under my breath. Later, I turned to the front of the news-sheet, and there I found the news of the Battle of Dysert O'Dea.

It read:

'Our Special Correspondent
~ Manus O'Heron ~

Battle of Dysert O'Dea.

he Earl of Essex's troops, under the leadership of Sir Richard De Clare, The Steward of the Forest of Essex [43 approx.], was brutally butchered by the wild Sons of Erin, under the leadership of a High King of Tara, Conchobhar O'Deaghaidh [45-ish] who are allied in revolt with the Scottish brothers Bruce.

The battle took place in the low swamp-like marshes near Corofin, in County Clare. Eyewitness' report that the Earl of Essex, Sir Walter Deveroux [49], had ordered De Clare meet the enemy and defend the castle at Bunratty.
De Clare divided his force into three columns and began the attack on the revolutionary forces early in the morning.
The first division was headed by de Clare's son, Gilbert [24], named after their ancestor 'Strongbow.'

I started, my interest keen.

' I know that chap! Strongbow,' I said to Sir Anatole.

'He was at the Battle of Lincoln Fair with me. When I was The Marshall's squire.'

Sir Anatole was nowhere to be seen. He had disappeared suddenly. The room was empty. I continued reading;

> '*Gilbert De Clare's forces moved quickly, to the north, to circle through the morning mists. The second column travelled southwards, to quell any support that may arrive, and to outflank the Sons of Erin. While De Clare himself led the main thrust on O'Dea's centre.*'

> '*The O'Dea's men used their local knowledge of the land, and their native magic to bring down the mists, and made their force appear smaller than they really were, and they slowly retreated, thus drawing the centre of De Clare's forces into the boggy, mist strewn, wetlands.*'

> '*The ambush came at about four bells, afore noon. The Normans were slaughtered, as O'Dea's troops fell on them from all sides, appearing as from nowhere like the very Jinn themselves. Hitting hard, and then vanishing…back into the heavy mists.*'

> '*De Clare was felled by an axe, cut*

clean, diagonally, from shoulder to teat. His head attached only by the slightest fold of skin. His son Gilbert died too, as the fighting became close, his body hacked and knifed by the Irish.'

'But alas, that's not the worst of it. As the Sons of Erin fell upon De Clare's retinue all who were not slain immediately, fell back to shelter within the tower of the keep.'

The O'Dea is a hard man. He has no need or indeed resource for a siege. Nor interest in ransom. Still, what followed was harsh; and reflects the nature of the wars in that divided land.'

'No parley took place. No parole was offered. The devil befouled enemy set fire to the whole tower. De Clare's wife perished in the flames, his whole line being extinguished by nightfall. Like a candle in the wind.'

'Credit; Manus O'Heron, Special Correspondent, Bunratty, Tara'

'Our correspondent Manus O'Heron, was truly appalled by this flagrant breach of the 'Code of War' and we, the editorial staff of the 'The Tears of Hermes' demand, on your behalf, that The King should

instigate reciprocal action immediately.'

~ The Editor. ~

14

The Meeting at the Nellie Dean

Sir Thomas Devereux; *has arrived, for his meeting with Strix, at the Nellie Dean, which stands on a small corner of Dean Street and Carlisle Street, Soho, London. W1D 3SU*

The Nellie Dean stands on a small corner where Dean Street and Carlisle Street meet. Strix was seated at his usual table. He sat in the corner of the room near the Carlisle Street entrance. His back was to the wall and he kept his eyes on both doors. We enacted a perfectly casual, chance encounter meeting. We had used the routine before.

I removed my cloak and loosened Red Feather from my belt, placing her on the stool next to me. I let a good four fingers of the blade out from the sheath and left it plainly on show. I rubbed my horse-sore buttocks carefully before I lowered them on to the three-legged stool, across the rough-hewn wooden table from him. Without any preamble, Strix began to explain to me what was happening. Chaos had erupted not only in my world but in the whole realm, and all whilst I had lain blissfully oblivious in the loving arms of my sweet Yvette.

'… After the farce of Bannockburn…'

Here I pulled a face and held up my hand.

'Please! Strix the memory is still too fresh. I was lucky to escape with my life.'

'Yes, be that as it may…His Grace is making his move now against the Lords Contrariants. They let him down so badly over that affair.' Strix stated.

'You mean they didn't turn up? Lancaster, and the rest of the boys…'

'Quite. The King is making his move against them…' Strix continued to explain.

'It's a wild roll of the dice I fear. Designed to force *casus belli*.'

He lifted his tankard quickly and drained it to the last drop.

'Your serving, I think,' he said as he passed it to me. I ordered for both of us and we were refilled from the jug by a buxom, freckle faced blonde with wild bushy hair who, answering my enquiry, told me with a wink and a smile, that her name was: 'Nellie of course.'

I laughed and said: 'I bet they are all called *Nellie*, don't you Strix?'

I know and keep Strix's secret on pain of his life and probably my own too. He took the refilled tankard, and raising it to the roof saying loudly: 'The King.'

And without further preamble, he launched into the meat of the story, as was his way.

'There has been bad blood between Isabelle, the queen consort, and the Baroness Badlesmere, Margaret de Clare, for some time. And the king means to use this, and more, to his own advantage. Recently, His Grace's spies,' he coughed and that portion of his cheek that could be seen above the hairline of his dark beard took on a pinkish glow.

' … His Grace's spies had learned that Badlesmere had relocated the whole of his fortune in the mighty keep of Leeds Castle, of which he is the custodian for the crown. The king strongly suspects, and I for one feel he is correct in his suspicions, that this fortune is collected for the sole purpose of funding a rebellion.'

'We all know that the Baron Badlesmere's affections have strayed from the king. And although he served his father, The Longshanks, well and faithfully, in both offices of the realm, and in the wars in the Old Possessions, the Colonies and against the Scots, I fear that he loves our new king not.'

He paused for a slurp before continuing.

'...And further, that he, Badlesmere, whilst letting it be known that he was visiting Pontefract; *on the business of his estates*...was in reality heading to Oxford, to meet with Lancaster and the Lords Contrariants.'

Another slurp.

'There are those that say the king eyes this treasure for his own use, but they are badly misjudging him. Though it is obvious that His Grace has need for more money - the perpetuation of the Great Empires wars, you understand, is an expensive business. Still, the investment will reap huge rewards in the near and far eastern empire, as well as in The Colonies.'
He slurped again.

'It is a clever ploy to use the women's enmity to force a move. I smell the sodomite, Piers Gaveston's hand here. It's far too bright an idea for the king himself. Maybe Isabelle has planned this move?' he said, cocking his head to one side.

'She has a sly cunning for such a young woman, to be sure. She is more of a fox, than a she-wolf, eh?'

'I would rather not smell Gaveston's hand, as I could never know exactly where his fingers had been.' I stated. Strix gave me a hard stare. He raised an eyebrow, looking like the owl on his seal ring, and ignored my quip entirely. There was a very serious air to Strix's demeanour, and for the remainder of the conversation we spoke softly with our heads together, there in the darkest corner of the room. It would be too easy for someone to shout *'treason!'* in these strange days. He spoke quietly in a soft whispered voice;

'Quite you fool. The inquisitors are everywhere! Remember; *The walls have ears and sometimes they have eyes too.'*

Then he continued: 'Isabelle was progressing to Canterbury, ostensibly to make a pilgrimage to the bones of poor murdered Thomas, may the Gods forgive Henry FitzEmpress…and she had decided to break her journey for the night at Leeds Castle. That is the story anyway.

'I myself however, have never found Isabelle to be such a devout woman. Apparently, she had not thought to send word ahead of her visit. It is normal practice to do so. Thus, allowing the custodian time to be able to provide her and her retinue, with accommodation, food, and fresh horses.

'But then again, as I have said, it is a royal castle and Badlesmere is only the steward and custodian, in His Grace's name and favour. However to arrive so, without notice, is most discourteous. Even for the Queen consort.'

He paused and looked about the inn. Then he drained his glass with a knowing look which left me in no doubt that I was to replenish the tankards. When this had been accomplished he continued.

'This is of course is the clever part of the plan. The women really do hate each other, as only women can. It relates back to a few separate incidents.' He held up a finger.

'*Primus*; The affair between the Queen and Richard de Clare. Richard is Margaret's elder brother and they were close as children. Of course you know Red Richard. Yes, he was with you at the battle of Lincoln. Was he not? The Queen liked to use Richard as her

paramour in his time at court. And whilst I am sure
he enjoyed their tryst enormously, for the Queen is a
woman of a voracious appetites, it was only a matter of time before her eye moved on to another. And
when it did, she rejected him outright.'

He picked up the refilled tankard and continued;

'In itself, a woman dominating the sexual dance is
something some men never like to experience. Yet
it is also something any man would eventually get
over, even a dullard like De Clare, given sufficient
time. Unfortunately, the Queen wanted to rid herself
of him quickly, to avoid any possible embarrassment
upon His Grace's unexpectedly hasty return from his
progression of the old possessions and so she arranged for Essex, your father, to remove Richard and
had him sent off to the war in Ireland.

'This obviously displeased the Baroness
Badlesmere, and whilst arguments ensued between
the two, it would, given a fresh wind, have all blown
out in time.'

'Like white clouds on a windy day.' I quoted a line
of prose from something I was working on. Strix
gave me a quizzical look before saying;

'*Secondus*; Later that year, Baroness Badlesmere
asked the Queen to appoint her nephew, Bartholomew de Burghersh to the office of the exchequer.
In a purely minor role. Still, one that would help
the lad's prospect for a good marriage. So important
nowadays, you know,' he said looking at me with
sad, thin eyes.

'The Queen, responded, and this in public too,
when she made a comment about the lad's parentage
and turned the proposition down flat; like honey,
being spread upon bread.' He lay his own quotation
like a trump over mine, winning the trick, before
shaking his long, scrawny, finger into the air, looking
like every teacher I had ever seen, and continuing:

'*Tertius*; The kidnapping. On her way from Caerle-on to Oxford, Margret was taken captive by a band of Welshmen, led by Owen the Red Hand, a small lord of the Welsh Marches. You will have heard the stories. They are common knowledge nowadays.'

I nodded in agreement: 'Quite a girl, what?'

Strix frowned at me and I could tell that things were serious, as he didn't even pause to berate me.

'And so…*Quartus*; The whole was compounded when Richard de Clare was killed at the battle of Dysert O'Dea, so recently. In all, battle and flame, perished eighty and more knights and nobles and some ten and four hundreds mounted and foot.'

Strix paused and looked about the tavern.

'Strange, the circle of time…'

15

Time And A Word

Sir Thomas Devereux; is meeting with Strix, at the Nellie Dean, which stands on a small corner of Dean Street and Carlisle Street, Soho, London. W1D 3SU

'Strange, the circle of time...' Strix paused for a few moments, thinking his peculiar thoughts, and then started to chunter.

'Time is such a strange thing. It's hard to put your finger on it. It is constantly shifting. It is hard to measure. My time is different to your time... It's difficult. You hear a horse come towards you...and then it passed, and you hear it still, as it moves away. Is time the same as sound? I asked John Dee once... he told me; '*You must remember that time is relevant, irreverent, and wholly in the eye of the beholder*'... what in the name of God's holy teeth, does that mean anyway?'

I was a bit disconcerted by him naming John Dee. I looked around but I couldn't see anyone who was listening to us. Nor anyone else who Strix could be addressing. I presumed that he was talking to himself again, which after all, is not so unusual nowadays.

'De Clare...de Clare's wife is Joan of Acre. Was the King's sister. A royal Princess of the Bloode. John foresaw her death. He told me that '*she will die in exactly the same way, by evil deeds and by fire, just as her descendant will.*' He waved his hands hysterically and looked at me, his eyes growing wide and mad again.

'How does that make sense? How could he know that? Know that a person's descendant will die in the same way as that person…as the ancestor. How could he know that?' He shook his head and took another mouthful.

'Who is this Joan of Arc?' I asked, trying to bring the conversation back to something that I could at least pretend to understand. All this talk of *'god's holy teeth'*, Dr Dee's mystic globe, the speculum I think it's called, and time. As if time were something that could be held in the palm of your hand. It was a bit confusing to a dullard like myself. And anyway, I had never heard of Joan of Arc.

'What…?' He looked at me as if I had distracted his thoughts.

'Oh… Acre. Not Arc. You have been to Acre you fool.'

And I had. It was part of my disastrous Outremer adventure, my crusade. I rubbed the scar on my right forearm automatically. He place his tankard on the table and shook his head, and then said, and I definitely got the feeling here that he was not talking to me at all;

'No, It's not explained in the Book of Soyga and … well, I'm getting ahead of myself. It is confusing sometimes.'

I shook my head again before realising that was wrong, and began nodding my agreement.

'Dee informs me that the timelines are broken… they flow and twist. Something is wrong with them you understand. It is something that he has seen in his speculum, about a witch and a warrior…or a witch and a child…maybe both. It really is all very unclear. It changes each time he observes them. And the warrior…'

He paused, looked at me more slowly, then shook

his head sadly.

'Not that there are many witches left. And even less soon, now Edward has set his Witchfinder loose. Still, I have heard it said that witches are always stealing children…Aren't they? Or is that the fairies and gypsies?'

His eyes rested on mine again. He stared at me very strangely. It felt like he was searching within me. Searching for an answer to a question that he did not want to ask. And just for a moment, I wondered if he was really losing his marbles. Then I remembered that this was Strix. And Strix had always been more than a little peculiar. He drank strongly and then said: 'No. She is called Joan of Acre…but it can't be the same person, can it? It is a different problem, I'm sure. Nothing to worry yourself about.'

Strix coughed and shook his head and shoulders, as if a shadow had passed over his grave and then, pulling himself together, he smiled and I watched as Nellie refilled our tankards once again and asked if we would like bread and cheese too. We ordered and Strix continued, with what I think was a little remorse.

'And so, what began as slight and envy, then moved to dislike and distrust, has now turned to hatred, enmity…and ruin.'

We ate lustily of the cheese and bread, which was delivered this time by a dark haired Nellie, and afterwards Strix continued with his story.

'Isabelle arrived at Leeds castle, which the Baron had left with only a small retinue. To find the castle so weakly defended…unusually good fortune, no?'

'And so, Margaret believing; *That all this is just a trick to steal mine husbands treasures and goods…*' ordered that *The gates be closed and barred. The portcullis be brought down, and the bridge drawn up.*'

'Not a greeting the queen would welcome.' I interjected.

'The Marshall was sent ahead to have the gates
opened, and when he delivered the demand, in the
name of Her Grace, received the reply; '*The Queen
must seek some other lodging, for I would not admit
anyone within the castle without an order from my lord
husband.*'

'But the Queen's men did not withdraw. The Queen
herself approached the outer barbican and upon
hearing this insult, became madder than a wet hen.
She ordered an assault upon the castle. And the Baroness, standing in full view proudly upon the bat-
tlements, responded by giving the order for arrows
to be loosed. Nineteen men were feathered, with six
dying from their wounds, including a young boy of
twelve, the Marshall's squire...'

'Hey... I was once the Marshall squire.'

Strix jerked his head up, and a spoonful of beer
slopped wildly from his tankard.

'Ye gods. I had forgotten that. Of course...I will
need to check that out immediately. Did the Marshall
have many squires?' he asked me, making note in a
little black book that suddenly appeared from up his
sleeve, with one of those new contraptions that he
called a carbon rod. He had gone as pale as Sir Rembald's white mare.

'*Now that was a bit weird, even for you Strix,*' I
thought, but I answered

'Well, John D' Erley, who, as everyone knows, has
been with the Marshall forever.' I said with a meaningful wink.

'Then there was me, but he lost me in the holy
lands...the wager with Sir Rembald...there was the
Bertrimon boy, I forget his given name, and there
had been young Anton Beauchamp, but no one ever
really talked about him. Before my time really.'

Strix sat for a moment, contemplating, and drank

another large mouthful of ale. He eyed me strangely again and looked pensive as he cleared his throat, before he said;

'That may be the breakthrough I have been searching for. Now where was I? Yes, and so began the battle of Leeds Castle which, as everybody knows is nowhere near the small mill town of Leeds and is actually two hundred and sixty odd miles away near Maidstone in Kent.' I spluttered in my beer at this last piece of information. Humour from Strix - he really must be cracking up after all.

'Anyway the king, of course, raised his banner against such an; *Ignoble act, and an insult to his Queen Consort.* And he gathered to him the nobles, including six earls, and all the support of the outraged populace, and within a day, a very short period of time for all to be made ready -no? The King's military expedition set off to crush the revolt; '*To avenge the grievous insult delivered to the queen by one of mine subjects.*'

'A relentless siege and numerous assaults using ballistas took place. Margaret, who was expecting the Earl of Lancaster with his force to arrive and relieve her, held out with her nephew, the aforementioned Bartholomew, and the small garrison of men. But after five days it became obvious that no relief would arrive and she yielded the castle to the King, receiving a promise of mercy from him.'

More drinking.

'And so, the King has gained possession of the castle, and more importantly, all the treasures within it. He hanged the Seneschal, and the twelve men of the garrison from the castle walls. A small group of knights, from nearby Whitney did arrive to give aid to Margaret...but it was too little, too late, and once they saw that the castle was taken, they claimed to have come to support the king.'

'Baron Badlesmere has fled. North of the Gap. They say he has sought refuge with his relative, the Bishop of Lincoln, at his palace of Stowe Park. Margaret, with her five children, and her nephew, were taken to the White Tower.'

'Good deer there.. Stowe' I said remembering the feast before the Battle of Lincoln Fair.

'The captives were made to walk all the way to the tower. Crowds of people turned out and harangued and insulted them as they passed, for maltreating their queen.'

Strix paused for a few heartbeats and looked around the room, taking in all who were there and thinking his strange thoughts. This time he did not drink. Slowly his thin eye fell upon me.

'His Grace has won the first battle. Now we must help him win the war.'

'We?' I stammered.

'Yes. We! You young scallywag. It is time for you to act as the man I know you can be. I need you in my service. It will give you the income you so desperately need. And it will stand you in good stead with His Grace. And that, in its turn, will solve the problem of your derivation. For now, after this tragic death of your brothers you have become an heir. In my service…and with the luck of the gods, I believe I can raise you high.'

I gulped and reddened. It was the first time my derivation had ever been mentioned outside of the family. And mentioned as if it was general knowledge too.

'My boy.' He coughed, embarrassed for me.

'It's not your shame…but even the poorest fool knows that a wife…a good wife…does not give forth issue when her husband is absent from her bed, separated by the mountains and sea, for well over a year and more. No. You have the name…but not the inheritance. That maybe something that His Grace can change.'

I hadn't ever really known it. Not as the truth. And yet I always had. It was plain that father could never stand to look at me. And as a child, we had met e*n famille* only a handful of times. I had always been pushed around the relations. Like a collection plate. Nobody really wants to…but they all chip in, if you get my meaning. It was not until I was a squire to the Templars, in Outremer, that anyone had mentioned it, and even then not to my face. But at Cambridge, there had been a nasty story about mother. And in Jerusalem, King Guy had refused to have me in the room. Saying that '*Such as I, was unfit for his presence.*'

Of course I was so young and naïve then, and didn't comprehend his meaning. I believed it was because I was not yet a knight. But the look of pity that Sir Rembald gave me was clear, and his shame for me was written across his face. And so here it was. Spoken aloud for the very first time.

'Ah, you know my hidden shame.'

16

Yorick Has A Premonition

Sir Thomas Devereux; is at the home of Lady Yvette Waterton, The Watermill, Axholme, which nestles in the bottom corner of Yorkshire, on the borders of Nottinghamshire and Lincolnshire, in that part of the Kingdom known as North of the Gap. DN10 6 HN

'I was so happy to see you. To know you are safe. I knew there had been deaths. I was warned. I…I thought that perhaps…' She paused and looked at me. I could tell that she had been crying.

'You thought that it was me who had died?' Yvette did not answer. She bent her head low, her shoulders sagged. I held her close and felt the sob as her body shook.

'Yorick, he had…a premonition. He foresaw that death's shadow had fallen upon the House of Devereux. And the rumours were wild.' The sobs became stronger.

'Oh Thom…I could not bear to lose you.'

I looked at Yorick as he sat by the fireside. He removed his pipe as his head turned towards the pair of us. His hollow eye sockets looked directly at me for the longest time. I was the first to break the stare. It was the only time I felt a dislike for the skeleton.

'Was your mother angry that you returned to me so quickly?' Yvette asked me as she regained control of herself and moved away from me. She began moving about the kitchen and tidying things away.

'Yes. No. Yes…she was but I really could stand to stay no longer. The tragedy of it all. I know it was heartfelt but it did seem as if mother was…she was so immersed in the mood. I am not good in situations like that. The family thing - I am not used to it. It doesn't really work when I am around. I just needed to get away.' Yvette thumped me in the chest. I could tell that she was shocked.

'That is a terrible thing to say! They were your brothers. Her children. It is only right that a mother should grieve. And your brother's young wife, the poor girl!' She started to sob again. I moved in and pulled her close. I held her tight.

'It's alright. I am safe. *We* are safe.'

Ferdinand the cat wound himself between our legs and began purring loudly, as he rubbed himself against us, his tail swishing back and forth.

'You will miss your brothers.' Yvette said after a few moments.

'Walter and Francis,' I felt a lump growing in my throat.

'… They are…were…my brothers but…I never really knew them…not *really* knew them. Not like I do Robert. They were brought up with father at Chartly, his castle in the Midlands, whilst I was brought up… well, wherever my mother's sisters happened to be or at Devereux House with my big sisters Penelope and Dorothy ruling over me.

'Then, at the first opportunity, father had me shipped off to school. We both know how that went,' I told her. I felt a little mean-spirited saying this but after all, it was true.

Walter had always treated me well and I liked him. He had a lively spirt about him. But Francis…he was more sullen. I hardly knew Francis at all. I got the feeling he resented me. We, as a family, only met at special occasions, like Christmas or the King's coronation. And still, somehow, I felt an emptiness, now that they were gone.

'I remember. You were a terror at school. That incident with the Archbishop!'

'Bishop. He was only a bishop then.' I explained. She laughed for the first time since I had arrived. The smile lit up her face, like the sun lights up the sky.

'This changes things Thom. Many things. Do you know what this will mean for you?' Yvette asked me, her eyes unable to hold mine, and she looked swiftly away. I saw Yorick stir and watch us with his unnerving gaze. He thought for a moment and then moved the queen knight to queen's bishop three.

'I don't honestly know. I haven't really thought it through. Strix was talking about it improving my chances in life. That seems unlikely to me. Father still resents me as much as he ever did. Possibly more now. Although he never really liked Walter much either...but Francis...Francis was his favourite. However, Strix did point out the fact that I am now, officially, the second in line to the inheritance. If you can be inline for an inheritance when you have been disinherited. It is not something I want to think about.'

'It is frightening how quickly a happy life can change,' she said looking into the distance. And, as if to emphasise her words, the sun slipped behind a cloud and a chill wind blew through the open kitchen door.

17

A Dead Man's Chest

Sir Thomas Devereux; is at the home of Lady Yvette Waterton, The Watermill, Axholme, which nestles in the bottom corner of Yorkshire, on the borders of Nottinghamshire and Lincolnshire, in that part of the Kingdom known as North of the Gap. DN10 6 HN

It was dusk now. We had spent a pleasant afternoon frolicking by the millpond which runs down by the vegetable garden. We had lain in the meadow, sipping wine, as the great wooden wheel of the mill creaked pleasantly and the canvas of the sails flapped in the gentle breeze.

Later Nosher, the scruffy urchin, appeared in a beaten up old dogcart, pulled by the sorriest nag that I have ever seen. He was delivering the box that Yvette had bought at the auction.

'You know, the box must be worth more than the boy's cart and nag together.' I dug into the pocket of my travel cloak that Yorick the skeleton, who sat in his corner, politely passed to me. I gave a coin to Yvette.

'Oh you are such an insufferable snob.' she replied, or some such, and told me that I should bring what was left of the wine, a really nice Nuis St George, from my grandsire's vines, and help her examine the contents.

'Of the bottle or the box?' She laughed. As I returned, Yvette was thanking the urchin and giving him a halfpenny for his trouble. The urchin gave me a curious glance, as if mine was a face that he needed to remember. I twisted my nose as he placed the box on the kitchen table and returned to his vehicle. It was then that I heard the most appalling noise. It seemed to emanate from the cart's, obviously illegal, sound system. He set off down the lane like the famous Charioteer of Delphi, the old nag showing a turn of speed that was unbelievable, scattering pebbles left and right, as he headed out of the gate.

'I will put a wager on that beast at the next tourney. That youth will go deaf. But only if the Inquisitors don't get him first. Oh, it's a real celestial box, lets open it up.'

Yvette opened the box and we took the contents out slowly. They were wrapped in soft cloths. She carefully unwrapped each one and placed them on to the kitchen table. The box itself was made of a hardwood with polished brass hinges and lock. It was intricately inlaid with ivory and jade. It contained the following; a dented brass plate, a delicate celestial vase with a crack in it, a carved wooden bowl and a broken bracelet with characters dangling from it, that I have heard people call charms. The ivory and jade carving on the lid displayed a red dragon in full flight. Not much to make such a fuss about you may think but I could see why Yvette liked it. It was about a cubit long and half that high.

'Look, there are symbols on the bowl, and there is one on the plate too.' Yvette commented.

'Yes?' I replied, taking the bowl and holding it nearer to the candle, so as to see the symbols in more detail.

'The symbols for the cross and the crown, the scimitar and the crescent moon, a pyramidal 'Eye of Providence', and a five sided star. Excellent. Excellent.'

'Oh, how clever you are Thom…and look, the vase also has a symbol.'

'That's a white lotus.' I informed her;

'And here on the box itself, is a cross pattée and see, upon the bracelet, the charms are symbols for the Earth, Fire, Water, Sun and Moon.'

I was going to continue but at that point Oda appeared at the window and tapped furiously upon the pane, with a rhythmic beat that surprised me. A few moments later the dogs began to bark. They were accompanied by the sound of horses in the yard. This was followed shortly by a hefty banging upon the front door. Yvette rushed over to the window and peaked through the hangings.

'Thom, it's the dibble!'

'The Sheriff, at this time of night? Yvette my dear, what have you been doing?' I gasped as I joined her and saw three men brandishing torches in the night air. Yvette came into my arms and kissed me gently.

'What me? I have done nothing that I should be ashamed of. Not yet anyway…' She smiled slyly, squeezing just above my inner thigh. I looked nervously at the door as the banging came again.

'Doesn't little Thomikin's want to stay then?' she said, in what I can only describe as a most seductive voice. Her lips turned from a pout into a smile , and she laughed as I stuttered and turned red.

'I'm only teasing you, silly,' then she patted my head, rather like she would have done to a little boy or a favoured dog.

'You really must go darling…I still have *so* much to accomplish… and…well they must not catch you here. These new cultural laws. I am breaking at least a dozen of them. And Strix…well, he needs you too.'

I started to say something in protest but placing her index finger across my lips she continued.

'I know darling but don't be foolish. I am in no danger. And you will only cause more trouble than either of us need. Best if I deal with these unwanted visitors myself.' She hesitated for a moment.

'They have been watching me for the last moon and more. So, quickly now away with you! Out of the backdoor and up the hill. Follow the line of hawthorne, then go across the meadow. Head for the Great North Road. Strawberry is waiting. Follow Oda, she knows the way.'

'Are you really sure? I can take them easily. There are only the three of them.'

She stamped her foot and pointed at the door.

'Yes. Well, thank you for an excellent stay. I love you. Always. You will be safe on your own?' I asked, as I kissed her again.

'Thom, you know that I am far from defenceless… and…oh darling, please be careful, you are in far more danger than I am. Go now. Please, I beg of you.'

Yvette pushed me towards the back door. I stole one last glance at the box and its contents, that were now laid out on the table, and felt my heart yearning. I wanted more time to study those symbols. They reminded me of something. Something that I felt was important. The banging came again. I heard Yvette shout as she headed down the short corridor.

'Who the hell are you to break down an honest woman's door? And in the middle of the night too. Declare yourselves now! Before I set the dogs on you!'

The smile on my face grew and I feared for the Sheriff as I heaved my getaway bag on to my shoulder, and headed for the floury inners of the Mill. Strawberry was waiting under the great oak. Tied to her saddle was a bag of food and a skin of wine. The same urchin who had brought the box stood there. He smiled inanely. Oda sat on a low branch, her head bobbing up and down, like a magpie's head will do.

'Here's Nosher,' the collection of dust, dung and straw stated mysteriously. He blinked his bright green eyes and waved me farewell with a flick of his hat. Strawberry strode steadily away, along the tree lined path, and south towards Nottingham.

It must have been an hour later that I began to wonder how Yvette had known to have Strawberry ready and waiting, and that I would need supplies, and why had it taken so long to deliver that damn box, and who exactly is this Nosher?

18

A Stranger in a Strange Land

Lady Yvette Waterton; *is at The Watermill, Axholme, which nestles in the bottom corner of Yorkshire, on the borders of Nottinghamshire and Lincolnshire, in that part of the Kingdom known as North of the Gap. DN10 6 HN*

You know that feeling you get sometimes? You are not quite sure why, because you can't actually see anyone, yet for some reason, you just feel that someone is watching you. Well, that was the feeling that I had right now, and I can tell you, I thought it might just be that Witchfinder and his *pricker* man again. Still the dogs were silent, and the hounds, who lay dreamily under the great oak, had not stirred.

It was a few days before Ascension and as still as a day can be. There was just enough of a gentle breeze to take the edge off the heat, and the early morning mist clung to the hedgerows. The grass was still damp, even though the sun was rising high now, about five bells in the forenoon. The river gave a laughing gurgle as the wheel of the mill turned smoothly, and the ambience of whole world had a gentle rhythm to it. I was out in the vegetable patch, weeding and hoeing, and getting the salads and greens, ready for the day's meal. That's when I had that feeling. And placing my hands on my back, as if it ached, slowly I raised my head.

Sure enough, there was someone watching me. But it was not who I had imagined it to be. In fact, if it had been a game of 'Who is the stranger at the door?' I am afraid that I would never have been able to guess. No, not even close. Not in a millennium.

You see the stranger was a monk. And, I would guess by the look of him, despite his shaven tonsure and his long grey, travel stained habit, a very young monk. He looked to be about eleven years old - perhaps a bit older, perhaps a bit younger, it's always hard to tell with boys of that age but he was thin, and straight with a good stance. Anyway, he was taller than Nosher, and obviously cleaner, even though he was covered in dust from the long days on the road.

'*Now here is a stranger in a strange land,*' I misquoted to myself.

'Hello stranger. Are you travelling far? Would you like some water or food?' I asked him.

'I am The Boy,' he said simply. And for a moment my heart stood still.

'I can offer you my labour to pay for the food,' he continued.

'Let us not worry about that just yet.' I responded, thinking '*No, It cant be...*'

'And I am Lady Waterton. You can call me Mistress Yvette. Come, it's nearly six bells a'forenoon anyway.'

'Yes, Mistress.'

We made our way towards the Watermill, moving through the garden. I stopped to wash my hands at the pump, and then walked through the open back door and into the big old kitchen. The Boy followed me to the well, washing as I did, and then came into the kitchen, all without saying a word. Yorick ceased puzzling over the chess board and stared at The Bo. The stare turned into a loose jawed fleshless smile. The kind of smile that all skeletons give to someone that have just met and like the look of. It radiated *bonhomie*.

The Boy, in his turn, did a double take when he saw Yorick but he said nothing, for he was far too well mannered to mention that fact that in the corner of the kitchen sat a skeleton, who had a black cloak draped over his shoulder, smoke an old clay pipe and appeared to be playing chess with himself.

'This is very like the abbey kitchen.' He said eventually.

'The abbey...now which abbey would that be I wonder?' I asked him.

'I am from the great abbey at Rievaulx. But I failed to give satisfaction, and have been banished for my heresies,' answered The Boy.

'Heresies eh.' I stated, raising an eyebrow and giving a puzzled smile. Yorick gave a slight rattle of his bones, as he too tried to raised an eyebrow.

'And where is it that you are heading to now?'

'I journey to the sister abbey at Revesby. I am to join the heretics there and do penance. Is it very far from here?'

'It's not far, and yet it is all the distance in the world.' I simply stated. I studied this Boy. Scrutinising him from head to toe. There was a familiarity about him that I found profoundly disturbing. The way he stood, with his head slightly to one side...

'No, It can't be... can it? It's just a legend... isn't it?' my inner voice asked.

Oda, my strange magpie, flew in through the open kitchen door. She landed on the table, near where Ferdinand was sleeping in a chair next to the fire, and she walked about in that awkward, agitated manner of hers. Ferdinand opened an eye, just a fraction, and yawned as he flicked his tail at her.

'Riiik-rak-rak-rak.' Said Oda, and I looked at her, as she nodded her head up and down frantically. The

Boy looked startled, and stared at Oda for a few moments, and then looked at me again, puzzled by the bird's appearance.

'Is - is this the same bird…that has travelled with me? Have I been led here?'

'Well… you will have to ask her that?'

The sun dropped behind a cloud and deep shadows spread across the room enveloping me completely. The fire crackled and hissed as I bent to stir the large black pot that bubbled and spat.

The Boy's eyes opened wide and I saw fear run across his face as he remembered every story that he had ever heard about the old crones that inhabited lonely isolated spots and what happened to the hapless strangers who venture near them, and were never seen again. I added a flickering of flakes to the grey mixture. Then picking up a large, long handled spoon I began singing the ancient washer woman's song;

> *'Hubble, rubble,*
> *What a muddle,*
> *Tumble dryer,*
> *And cauldron bubble…'*

19

The Foundling

Lady Yvette Waterton; *is at The Watermill, Axholme, which nestles in the bottom corner of Yorkshire, on the borders of Nottinghamshire and Lincolnshire, in that part of the Kingdom known as North of the Gap. DN10 6 HN*

Oda winked at us and hopped down to the floor. She continued her pacing. I replaced the lid on the laundry pot, and took a hot loaf from the range, bringing it to the table, and cutting a large wedge, placed it on a platter. I handed it to The Boy, along with a knife. Then bringing the cheese from the cold store I placed it on the table next to the bowl of apples.

'I can offer you ale, or milk, which would you prefer?' I asked him, wondering again about his age.

'I believe milk will be the best choice,' he said after consideration; He took his time as if he had never been given a choice before.

'I have never partaken of the ale, although the monks are master brewers. It was frowned upon for all but the highest to partake. Although Brother Ignatius, the Brew Master, was renown for his…indulgences.' He laughed with a huge grin, and suddenly the sun shone through the door, bright and dazzling.

'Were you at the abbey long?'

'All my life.' replied The Boy;

'And I expected to stay and take the holy orders, or maybe even join the Templar's as a novice, but alas, I am accursed.'

'Accursed, banished, and you…so young. You certainly have started a big adventure haven't you? And after all, entirely the most important thing about an adventure is to start it.'

He ate lustily, as all young boys do, and I used the time to study him further.

'So have you always been called The Boy?' I asked him as I poured him some more milk.

'Yes. I was a foundling and delivered to the gates of the abbey. I am not to be named until I take the vow.'

I nearly dropped the beaker, as I turned to look at The Boy even more closely.

'F-Foundlings…are rare nowadays.' I said shakily before asking;

'How old were you when you were found?'

'I was a new born babe. I am of eleven years or close to that I believe, and I was to take the holy vow next spring.'

Yorick rattled his bones and dropped a black bishop, his jawbone dropping at least an inch. Oda flew into the air, squawking loudly, before landing on the table. That is when I dropped the beaker of milk. It spilled all over the floor and finally Ferdinand oozed to life, a shiver ran down his body, before he busily began lapping at the milk. Oda surreptitiously stole bits of bread. Yorick became even more slack-jawed and I just fussed about cleaning up, trying to look nonchalant, and doing nothing useful at all, whilst I tried to recover my composure.

'So…Boy…the foundling heretic…what makes you so accursed?'

'*Try not to let yourself shake with anticipation*' my inner-self screamed at me.

'I have the mark of the devil.' He stated simply;

'The abbot hoped to cleanse me but I am beyond even his help.'

'And tell me…what mark would be so extraordinary, as to be beyond the help of the illustrious Abbot of Rievaulx, the brother of Kings, and a friend to the Pope?' I asked him.

'I have an extra nipple. The devil's own nipple. When he comes for me, that is where he will suckle. A third nipple. It is a sure sign of the evil within me.'

That was when I dropped my platter. Ferdinand looked at me with disgust and, leaping onto the windowsill, headed out into the garden, whilst Oda screeched and took to the rafters. Yorick said nothing but he did give me a very black stare.

'Goodness, I am a nervous Nellie today. Please forgive me. Help yourself to more bread and cheese, and there are some pickles too in the dresser. I have just remembered that I need to see to something…'

And I left the room in a hurry. I was frightened, scared, excited, and horrified, all in a moment. I ran to the solar and shut the door behind me. It is not often that I take a strong drink during the day, unless I am encouraging Thom to seduce me again, but today I thought that a swift glass of the old Irish, may just be what the doctor ordered. I swallowed quickly, and then had a second, slower mouthful. Placing the goblet on the table I took some parchment and smoothed it out. Then I raised the quill from the inkwell and started to write. It was a quick note and did not take long.

Thom,
It's The Boy. Here…
He is here in the kitchen!
You must get here and with all speed,
Before the Dibble or the Witchprick-

I wrote another letter, this one to Strix, before I left the room, and walked through the open windows that led to the garden proper. I whistled sharply. Oda and Ferdinand both joined me within a few moments. And I gave them instructions.

'Oda send the word, have the Tiding watch for the dibble, or worse! And watch the southern roads for strangers.'

'Quark, quark.' She flew.

'Ferdinand my old friend. I know how much you hate the water, but I will need you to travel to send the word. They must be warned. The canals will be safest. Head to Axholme, seek a boat heading west, yes, make sure that you are seen too, and then, at the last minute take one heading south. You must find them. This is urgent!'

He wrapped himself around my leg for a few moments, purring loudly, before he mooched away, as if he had not a care in the world. I held the notes up to my brow and searched the sky for Oda. She was gone.

Nosher stepped out of the bushes, his bight green eyes shining in the sunlight.

'Here's Nosher.'

20

All Tomorrow's Parties

Sir Thomas Devereux; is in his rooms above the emporium of Messrs Camden and Sons, by royal warrant and appointment to his gracious majesty Edward II, Royal Astronomers, Astrologers, Cartographers, Chart Makers, Horologist, Navigators, Oikouménê, Scribists, and who are of the Worshipful Company of Painter-Stainers and Sporting Bookmakers, which is situated in Neal's Yard, London. NC2H 9DP

I could already hear the soft strains of music floating upwards through the floorboards. It mixed easily with the booming of male voices and the hesitant laughter. Only a few days had passed since I had returned to the metropolis. As I laced up my doublet I was starting to feel that slight unease - the feeling that I always get just before I have to commit to any form of social engagement that involves leaving the homestead especially if it involves meeting other people.

Shyness had never been a problem for me but, after my crusade, and Hattin in particular, I did feel more comfortable on my own, at home, or with my dear Yvette. But I couldn't let the Camden brothers down…could I?

I was just thinking of some way of weaselling out when Sir Anatole staggered in to the room. He collided with the table, and then knocked over a stool,

before falling face downwards on the floor in a shabby, drunken pile. My decision was made for me. The
very idea of spending an evening with his rotting
corpse was really beyond the pale. And so, checking
my reflection in the tarnished copper kettle, I strode
manfully down the stairs that led to the yard, and
within three strides I was at the front door of their
emporium.

Messr's Camden and sons held these little soirees
of theirs from time to time. Todays was to celebrate
Ascension, which just happened to coincide with the
unveiling of their impressive new map of the world.
Their invited guests ranged from the high and
mighty of the realm to the notable of the scientific
community, sprinkled with a scattering of import
naval officers. I had the feeling that I was only invited because I was behind with the rent, and it gave
them the opportunity to keep their collective eye on
me.

A man, obviously not a butler, but definitely some
one who does-for, met me at the door and asked;

'What name is it, Sire?' And on my reply said: 'The
master is expecting you M'Lord, please follow me
into the small library.' I did; and he announced me
with ringing tones. Of course he got it all wrong. I
am not, and never shall be a Lord. Mister Sampson
Camden, the senior of the brothers, rushed forward
to greet me.

'My dear chap, how wonderful of you to attend…
such a great honour…please…please let me provide
you with a sherry that we have specially,' he coughed
and looked embarrassed.

'It's imported from Porto…most fine. I must express my deepest sympathy…I did not know your
brothers but William did. We had a very sad letter
from him…terrible, just terrible.' He paused and let
his big bovine eyes blink uneasily at me for a mo-

ment before continuing;

'I believe you know Doctor Sopenhiemer, the judge?'

He left me with an awful sherry, and a small fat man.

'Hello Soapy, how the devil are you? I see you have been feasting again,' I said to Soapy.

'Dev, how unexpected. Are you still charging around the country in chainmail? I thought you might have had enough of that palaver - it's not good for the health you know.

Just look at De Clare. They chopped him into little pieces. His wife and son too. No - if I were you I would concentrate on finding yourself a wife.'

He launched into his spiel about a wife being a good thing for a man. And I swallowed it, and washed it down with the sherry.

'Let me ditch this poison and see if anything more suitable is available,' I said when I got the opportunity.

For those of you who are new to my society, you may not have met Soapy before, but Soapy, Sudsy, Joe the Soap, or to give him his correct title, Doctor Joseph Sopenhiemer, King's Councillor, Doctor of Philosophy and Master of Arts, is an old friend of the family. I have known him since the distant school days of yesteryear.

Way back, in the cradle of our youth, we had terrorised quite a few of the smaller villages of middle England with our wild antics. Now of course, Soapy is the youngest of the King's Councillors, and acts as an advisor to his uncle who is a royal judge. He is quite a success apparently, which is something mother points out on a regular basis. Of course when I knew him best he was just a spotty oik from London Town, whose father was something in the ministry.

'Are you still lazing about the place, pretending to write, and slipping your hand into your mother's purse?' He asked me as I handed him a glass of Irish whiskey, newly smuggled from Dublin to Bristol, and down the Avon and Kennet canal.

'Why yes, and are you still clerking for your uncle?' I parried. These things always go the same way.

After you belittle each other for a while you move on to reminisce about the good old schooldays, which, as we all know, were universally hated, and then you move on again to old acquaintances, who are not present, and belittle them in turn.

We were just reaching that stage when who should turn up? Well you will never believe it, but none other than Bonzo. You know Bonzo?

Everyone knows Bonzo. About six and a half feet tall and so thin that he weighs absolutely nothing; even when he is sopping wet. He has long greasy hair, a face full of spots, and now-a-days sports a small moustache. When he turns sideways, he absolutely disappears from view. He claims, as a matter of fact, that this skill once saved his life in battle. The archers of Frankia being unable to distinguish between him and the rain, as it fell in straight lines.

Anyway, Bonzo is always immaculately dressed, and tonight was no exception. He was dressed entirely in rich red silks, a doublet and hose combination, with a racy shoulder cape, knee length black leather boots and the biggest hat I have ever seen outside of a racecourse on Ladies' Day. He looked like an embarrassed toadstool.

During our formative years Bonzo and I had indulged, rather too heavily some would say, in the better things that life has to offer. You know the kind of thing I mean. Late nights, wine, a good play, a bad play, more wine, the odd race card here and there, the tourneys of course, and once or twice a rollicking good concert. In fact, it was often said that, '*Where one of us went, the other was bound to be.*' And so it often proved.

Well that was in our youth, and is a story that we can save for another day. Nowadays, Bonzo is Professor Barrington Browne of St Catherine's College, Cambridge. What followed in the way of conversation went something like this:

'Well bless my soul, if its not old Dev!' on the one part, followed swiftly by;

'As I live and breathe, Bonzo Barrington Browne.' on the other. Along with lots of hand clasping, back slapping and general;

'Well I never…may the Gods' bless me… and who would have thought's…'

Once these pleasantries were over, I suggested that we head to the table in the corner where the alcohol was stored, and which seemed to be the centre of social attention. Of course Bonzo knows Soapy. Everyone knowing everyone in England. I mean, after all, *the Companions of the Conqueror*, and all that.

21

Companions of the Conqueror

Sir Thomas Devereux; is attending a celebration of Ascension with the Messrs Camden and Sons, by royal warrant and appointment to his gracious majesty Edward II, Royal Astronomers, Astrologers, Cartographers, Chart Makers, Horologist, Navigators, Oikouménê, Scribists, and who are of the Worshipful Company of Painter-Stainers and Sporting Bookmakers, held at their premises in Neal's Yard, London. NC2H 9DP

The thing is, that in England these days there is a section of the population to which Soapy, Bonzo, and myself, along with several hundred other young men belong. We are the sons that nobody knows what to do with. The leftovers after the feast.

You see what a member of the aristocracy really needs is an heir. Yes, an heir is imperative for the continuation of the line. Then a second son is fine, just in case the first happens to get killed in a tourney or hunting accident or some such. A third son can always be pushed into the church. Then you simply fill the place up with a few girls, who you intend to marry off to good advantage and that is it, your family life is all sorted out.

Unfortunately we are the fourth sons and a bit of a problem. You see there is no land available for us and it is unlikely, unless we get a good marriage, that we will ever amount to much. Still, they can't just ignore us entirely. So they send us off to school. Then they normally stick us into the army, hoping we will be killed off at the end of act one, as I've heard Marlowe put it. If the chap has a brain of any sorts, there are always the universities, and if not commerce and the Far East Company [incorporating India and Siam], who always keep an eye out for the bright young things. Failing that, they are more or less stuck with a young man hanging around the place all day, taking up space that could be used for something better, and forever dipping their sticky fingers in to the old treasure chest, and generally eating everyone out of house and home.

If you ask me frankly, that is why the mater and pater were so keen on the idea of the Templars. And then there was Bannockburn. I mean, what are the odds of a chap returning from that fiasco, eh? I suppose the Messrs Camden would know. Still we struggle along, and so here we all were; Bonzo, Soapy, and myself, and we were '*shooting arrows at the clouds*' as we always do, when I asked Bonzo;

'What the devil are you doing here? Awfully nice to see you and all that…but a bit of a surprise?'

Well, the long and short of it is Camden Brothers had very kindly asked him;

'*If he had nothing better to do, why not pop along about eight bells of the last dog watch to our little soiree, this very evening, where we will be unveiling one of our new maps of the land that lay beyond the Arctic Circle and The North East Passage. Dress informal.*'

The evening began to stretch out before us and we settled down to devour old Camden's Irish imports, and a good time was in the offing when… well…that's was when it happened, just as it always does, and against all the codes of good behaviour… some old decrepit rudely butts into our conversation.

'Please forgive my interruption,' says he, and without waiting for a reply continues, 'Did I hear you correctly? You did mention that you had a Chinese lacquered box and a vase from the T'Ang dynasty?'

Bonzo unfortunately, being socially insecure, has not yet developed the skills that we of the old guard have over the years perfected. Those skills that allow you to totally ignore a fellow, without hardly being rude at all. Well maybe just a smidgen, just for the hell of it. And so it was he, who replied; 'Yes, that's right. It belongs to my good friend here. We think that it maybe from the T'Ang dynasty...but we don't really know.'

'I know.' I stated looking as regal as a nobody can.

'Both the box and vase *are* of the T'Ang dynasty.' I stressed.

'Oh good, good...' said the decrepit one;.

'You may not know it but I have been studying the T'Ang dynasty for some twenty and more years now.' And he paused to slurp some more sherry from his glass.

'I'm always delighted when I come across anything that is related to the period. I've been writing a book on the subject, I seem to have been at it,forever... alas.' He shook his head sadly;

'Johanssons, the publishers, you know, are giving me hell. I seemed to have missed yet another dead-line or something. I just can't seem to get to the end of it.'

'*I know how he feels.*' I thought. My heart had begun to thaw at the mention of Johanssons, they being my own publishers, and this making him as near a brother to me as he was ever likely to get. Quite a dangerous thing at the moment.

'I don't suppose that you have this vase with you, do you, eh?' He continued.

'I am afraid that the vase is in my apartment.'I an-swered simply.

'Such a shame, I would love to see it sometime.' The eavesdropper said pleadingly.

'Your rooms are only upstairs,' interjected Bonzo in his thick-headed way.

'Oh good, let's go take a look at it then,' the decrepit one insisted.

'You don't mean now…this instant?' I replied.

'Oh, yes. The sooner the better,' came the answer.

'It's OK. Professor Witherspoon was up at 'Catz' with me and he is at Pembroke now, if I'm not mistaken. I can take him along if you like.' Bonzo commented. I couldn't help but smile as the decrepit one took hold of his arm and, pulling him rather too close, led him away.

'Goody-goody…' I heard him say as he disappeared from the room.

I wandered over to the drinks table and there found the Messrs Camden. Before I could say anything the younger, taller, brother Manoah spoke up;

'I see old Witherspoon collared your friend.' He raised his glass and beamed;

'Ah, Witherspoon leaving us so soon, I do hope you have enjoyed yourself?'

'Absolutely wonderful, my dear chap. Wonderful. However, it appears that this strappingly handsome young man has a vase for me to examine. I do hope that it's a big one. Please excuse us, Gentlemen. Goodnight,' said the decrepit one, surreptitiously squeezing Bonzo buttocks as he shuffled him through the door. Bonzo had started to look uncomfortable but he was out of the door before he could make a comment. Only his look shouted: *May the Gods protect me!*

'I say…I do hope your young friend will be all right with Witherspoon. He's a bit of a one for the young chaps.'

'Oh, I'm sure Bonzo can handle him all right.' I replied swallowing more whiskey.

'Yes, that could be exactly what Witherspoon is expecting,' smiled the younger of the Messrs Camden brothers as he sauntered away.

22

The Professor of Sinology

Sir Thomas Devereux; *is in his rooms above the emporium of Messrs Camden and Sons, by royal warrant and appointment to his gracious majesty Edward II, Royal Astronomers, Astrologers, Cartographers, Chart Makers, Horologist, Navigators, Oikouménê, Scribists, and who are of the Worshipful Company of Painter-Stainers and Sporting Bookmakers, which is situated in Neal's Yard, London. WC2H 9DP*

About a week after the Messrs Camden's party, I was at the old homestead, and, as is usual, I was up and about quite early.

It was precisely the stroke of the fifth bell of the forenoon watch. I was pottering around the kitchen, and having already made a pot of coffee, was debating with myself whether to have toast and strawberry jam or to nip down to Neal's Yard and get some croissants. I decided on the toast and strawberry jam, as I was feeling far too lazy to dress. And so, it was with toast in hand and coffee in cup, that I sat in the window seat and watched the morning unfold.

It was then, that I spotted yesterdays copy of '*The Tears...*' that Sir Anatole must have brought home. I picked it up and started to peruse its pages in search of the sporting news. There was an article on the famous Haxey Hood, which had been recently been run across the Isle of Axholme. Yvette had introduced me to the sport, and last year, she had persuaded me to enter on behalf of the Epworth Tap's team.

Well, of course, as a man recently returned from the crusades it would have seemed cowardly to refuse. What she had failed to tell me was that the 'Hood' was run from the Mowbray Stone, outside the local church, across ten and three miles of open countryside. And further that each of the nearby hostelries entered a team comprising of local able bodied men. The aim of the game was to capture the hood, a small leather parcel, and return it to your own hostelry. Now, I don't know if you are familiar with Axholme but there are a lot of hostelries in the environs of Epworth. And so in total several hundred men, a small army in truth, turned out to struggle for ten or more bells to win the honours. There is only one rule; No weapons are allowed. However, that didn't stop eight men from being killed in the crush.

Anyway, according to the broadsheet, this year it had been a close run thing, with The Duke William, The Kings Arms, The Red Lion, The White Bear, The Carpenter's Arms, The Fighting Cock, The Black Bull, The White Swan, The Mowbray Arms, The Crown, the Three Horseshoes, The Reindeer Inn and The White Hart all vying for the honours.

The article explained that the tradition stretched back to the first Lady de Mowbray, one of Yvette's ancestors, who, whilst out riding had lost her cloak hood to the strong winds. A couple of sons of the soil, seeing her in distress, chased after it, fighting for the honour, and the reward, of returning it to her. Why they had to '*smoke the fool*' by hanging him over a bonfire until he passed out, was never properly explained to me, but apparently he was allowed to kiss every girl he met that day. So, not a bad job really. Still as an ex-combatant, and loyal member of the Epworth team, I took a keen interest in the article.

Now, when I'm at home it is my choice to have about me as much noise or as little noise as I like. My choice today was noise. So my secret, wax cylinder sound system, was emitting a piece by my favourite music by Mr. Eddie *'Cleanhead'* Vinson.

These damned new Culture Laws are rather restrictive in their aim to control the population and the section on music and performance is particularly irksome and somewhat severely enforced by the ministry. One of my favourite poets, The Infamous Libertine, had recent run afoul of these laws and is now believed to be in hiding somewhere North of the Gap. However, in practise, we all ignored the Cultural Laws at every opportunity, and for those in the know it's easy to attend a secret underground performance. Such events are occurring with a growing frequency in both the town and the country.

And so, it was to the wholly illicit *Kidney Stew*, that I sat and perused the news of the last week.

After the sporting pages, I usually turn to the front of the newsheet and work my way through to the crossword. Sometimes I don't though and, for some reason, today was one of those days. I was working my way backwards and was moving from the 'Personal Requirements' section to the the bit called 'What's Occurring' and onto the local news, the bigger items of news having been splashed, as they say, on pages one to four, at the front. Well, here I was on page six, reading an article about a distinguished Professor of Sinology, and just as Eddie *'Cleanhead'* Vinson sang;

'She ain't the caviar kind, just plain ol' kidney stew,' when bells started to ring.

Not on the wax cylinder you understand, as next comes the saxophone solo, nor, I should say, out across Neal's Yard, but here inside the old noggin. Alarm bells. Bloody great big bells. Bells as big as Big Ben, the newly cast giant bell of Westminster Cathedral.

How many Professors of Sinology called Witherspoon can there be? And how many of them could be found dead in Cambridge? Dressing hastily, I rushed down the stairs that lead to the street and into Messrs Camden and Sons emporium.

'Good Morning Sire,' said old Sam Camden.

'Can we be of assistance? You wouldn't have come to pay the rent would you? No, off course not - please excuse my being indelicate…I'm sure Her Grace will oblige in due course.'

'He's copped it.' I stated simply;

'Right across the noggin. A poker the Inquisitor chap reckons. I can't fathom it myself. Why old Withers'? Harmless enough…the Inquisitor chap thinks there may be a scandal. A love triangle he says. They are interrogating Garce Holdem-Downe. One of Witherspoon's young sodomites it appears. I went to school with him. In Lincoln. Holdem-Downe I mean, not Witherspoon.' And I pushed the newsheet into old Sam's face.

'My goodness.

'Yes, we had the news yesterday. Most incommodité. I do hope the gentleman friend of yours, the Honourable Cedric Barrington Browne has not been injured too,' responded old Sampson in his overly polite manner.

'Bonzo? I had forgotten about Bonzo.' And in truth I had.

'Well it sounds to me as if I had better find out what has been happening.'

I set off to see if I could find Bonzo. I headed up to Charring Cross, down Old Compton Street and into Wardour Street and, after visiting several establishments, I found him in the Intrepid Fox and here I got my second surprise of the day, for Bonzo was talking with Strix, and I didn't know they knew each other. Strix and Bonzo both looked at me as I made my hurried entrance and Bonzo stood and said simply;

'Not now Dev…sorry, I have to flee.'

And he did, out of the Peter Street entrance, leaving Strix seated at the table in the corner of the room with his back to the wall and his eyes on both doors. He motioned that I should join him with a simple wave of his hand and upturned palm.

'Well met young Devereux,' he smiled;

'Most opportune…I take it you are seeking information with regard to the late Professor Witherspoon. I was just gathering some of the relevant facts from your dear friend, the Honourable Barrington Browne.'

Despite the fact that he could plainly see that I was bubbling over with questions, Strix held his finger up, indicating that I should remain silent for a few more moments and then continued;

'The honourable gentleman and I have been acquaintances since you were both up at Cambridge, and…he has been helping me with some of my inquiries, with reference to a certain foreign dignitary, who has been in the kingdom now for a good six turns of the moon and, during that time, there have been a number of bizarre incidents. They could conceivably be connected, in one way and another. You yourself also being one of the factors of my inquiry.'

'Wha…' I bubbled, but Strix continued to talk over me.

'You may recall the body in Camden Lock that I had you investigate. What you may not be aware of is the recent discovery of yet another body, which has been found in the Thames, with exacting similarities, and we feel - I feel that is, that these incidents are all

linked to the same organisation. And all are potential threats to the realm. And to the empire. Tell me
Thomas, what do you recall of the vase that your
friend…? ' And he coughed here.
'…Mistress Waterton acquired?'

23

The Intrepid Fox

Sir Thomas Devereux; is in secret conference with the mysterious Dr John Dee. They sit in a dark corner of the Intrepid Fox, which itself sits on the dark corner of Wardour Street and Peter Street, Soho, London, W1D 6QF.

'...I need you to locate that bargee you interviewed. I believe that you maybe on the right track there. This interest of yours in tattoos is most fortunate, yes indeed.

'This is only one thread of an international mystery and yet, still more important and urgent, are yesterday's events in Cambridge,' John told me.

'I believe that the Murder of Professor Witherspoon could be another thread of the same mystery? You will accompany me to Cambridge. We will leave in a few hours. I will meet you at Camden Lock. We must see this heinous crime for ourselves. We will visit old Witherspoon's apartments, I don't expect to find much of interest but it may be worthwhile...' He took a long drink.

'Who would want to kill old Withers'?' I asked. I was stunned by his death and genuinely puzzled.

'He *was* a weird fish...but we all have our oddities... but to kill him for his... hobbies, his indulgences, is simply...crass.' I said to John.

He nodded his agreement and finished his short beer. I knew it was a signal to me to refill the tankards and I ordered from the serving man.

'Crass indeed.' John agreed, accepting the refilled tankard.

'Let us consider who would want this death - who would benefit from it?' He looked thoughtful for a few moments before drawing a small leather-bound black book from his sleeve, and starting to scribble notes. He used his new carbon filled feather. He made a list, and as he wrote, we discussed the points:

Primus; Garce Holdem-Downe ~ His lover.
'If there has been an argument between lovers...' he wrote.

Secondus; His family ~
'There may be titles, land or even an inheritance. Many a nephew has sought to improve his situation by hastening the departure of an ageing uncle. And we should not ignore the distaff side of the family... but in this particular case it seems unlikely, from what I have heard of the crime. Unlikely...yet not impossible.'

'What have you heard?' I asked him but he ignored my question, raising an eyebrow, and continued to write.

Tertius; The Treasure of the T'Ang ~
'This theory of his about the Treasure of the T'Ang...there have long been rumours... Dr Dee will tell you much more. It is a special interest of his. You should speak with him,' he said.

'I will. But could it really be possible? Do you seriously suggest that Old Witherspoon could have been killed because of the vase...the vase that Yvette bought? What are the odds?' I interrupted him in mid-flow.

'I am sure that the Messrs Camden would give you

tight odds. It is far more probable that you think. The search for this treasure whilst the stuff of legend… is none the less real and each of the great powers has an interest in it. Each has sought…are searching… for this fabulous wealth. There are rumours that the treasure has been found…and that it was then stolen by a rebel warlord and carried across the steppes, along the Silk Road. And that it is now hidden deep in the high mountains somewhere on the borders of The Holy Roman Empire…Germania.

If that is so, it would explain some of the recent events in those principalities…and the results would indeed change the balance of power. And so that would give us…let me think…' He tapped the feather against his lips before continuing to write;

Anjou, Hibernia, Espana, Frankia,
The Holy Roman Empire, The Colonies,
and the Oriental Empire.

'These would be the prime movers but a whole host of secondary powers would also be interested. And we can not rule them out,' he commented before continuing.

'Anjou ~ they have their spies. You know one I think?'

'You don't mean…Sir Anatole?' I asked him disbelievingly, my voice hitting a semiquaver in high C with an added bit of reverberation, which gave it an amazing top spin.

'The very same. Did you not think it strange that he should move into your rooms just as you start to become useful again?'

I said nothing. I was in awe of this man. A beacon, a veritable lighthouse of knowledge. That he could know things that where truly obscure to me and yet seemed so obvious, once he had shone his light upon them.

'And the other powers could easily be using the same men, Sir Anatole, this Garce fellow or others perhaps…even professional killers. They could also be using their own spies of whom I know nothing.' He took time to order some cheese and bread.

'And so… ' He began to write again;

> *Quartus; Other Possibilities ~*
> *The King, Lancaster and his Nobles,*
> *The Pope's Church,*
> *Queen Isabella [with /without Frankia],*
> *Others unknown such as The Freethinkers,*
> *The Earls and Lords; like Drake, Mortimer,*
> *Young Bess, Mary of Valois, Lady Grey…'*

He paused and watched me for a long moment. Then he wrote;

> *Quintus; Anyone else ~*

He looks at me again, keeping his eyes on mine, then added;
Barrington ~ Browne.

He looked at me thoughtfully while I took in this last addendum.

'All would grab at the opportunity…and all would be acting through intermediaries, thus concealing their intent from those eyes that watch. It is time for you to shine my boy. I hope that you have kept that blade of yours sharp.' He looked at Red Feather keenly. I nodded. And silence folded around us and a small time passed.

'On second thoughts…the bargee is not your first port of call at all, if you will excuse the pun. But *do* have a quick word with Johanssons, will you? Yes…

the Professor wrote for their publication you know…
The Sinologist."

I knew that John meant that I was to send a message to a gentleman of my acquaintance, deep in the east of London Town. Bethnal Green to be accurate, Arnold Circus, E2 to be precise.

And that is what I did. Whilst I was waiting for Strawberry to be made ready, I scribbled a quick note to Johanssons which I gave with a few pence to a runner, who was doing precisely the opposite, as he lazed around the stables. More money changed hands at Camden Lock, and I was informed by an old man who kept his boat permanently moored there, that a bargee called Robyn, had set-off for Oxford, not two days past.

'Well barges can only go where the canal takes them, and they don't travel very fast. And if she were here two days ago, it seems unlikely that she was involved in the Cambridge murder. Yes…unlikely, but not at all impossible.' I said to Strawberry, as I patted her long nose. She whinnied her approval.

'We are to wait here for John. The Holloway Road is but a stone's throw away, and then we will follow the River Lea across country to Cambridge. We will catch up with the barge later.'

24

Sherlock Court

Sir Thomas Devereux; is with Doctor John Dee, when they meet Richard Topcliffe, the Inquisitor, and Doctor Niall Ó'Glacáin, the renowned medical surgeon, in the rooms of Professor Witherspoon, which are located in Sherlock Court, St Catherine's College, Cambridge. CB2 1RL

Strawberry and I were waiting for Strix outside the Devil's Cauldron, the famous music venue that stands on Camden Lock. The venue had been recently closed under the new cultural laws. My friends and I had spent many a happy hour there bopping the evening away. As I waited for John, I recalled some of the performers I had seen play here; The famous Stomping Mandolins, who still appeared regularly on the underground circuit, The Infamous Libertine, a scoundrel and poet, who is rumoured to be in hiding somewhere, possibly north of the Gap. A royal warrant for his arrest was pasted to the Cauldron's door. Some wit had painted eye-lenses and a moustache on it. And of course there was the most memorable night where, Bonzo, Soapy, and I had revelled to the music of the late, lamented, Stormy Clouds, the Hibernian Bard, and his incredible band, The Thunder.

Stormy always appeared with his bruised and battered five string lute, which he plugged in to his wondrous steam operated Sheriff's Sound Expander. It had been a great show. The greatest of all time. Unfortunately also his last. The Sound Expander exploded, sucking him into a vortex, and he disappeared, right there on the stage, with a whoosh and a bang. Oh…what a night, what a show, the grande finale. What a way to go! I know he would have loved every moment.

> *Tattoo'd lady*
>
> *Tattoo'd lady,*
> *Bearded baby,*
> *They're my family.*
> *When I was lonely,*
> *Something told me, where,*
> *I could always be.*
> *Where I could,*
> *Wish for pennies,*
> *If we had any.*
> *You'd meet me down,*
> *At the shooting gallery.*
> *Yes I'm a,*
> *Fairground baby.*
> *Wonder what made me,*
> *Fall for the pearly queen.*

I was wondering, for the umpteenth time, what a 'shooting gallery' was when a carriage pulled up. Its door swung open and the voice of Dr John Dee sang out.

'Wel-l-l…did you ev-e-r…?' It could not have been more perfect unless Stormy himself had sung it and finished with a crashing chord strummed on his famous lute. We both smiled at the memory. It has slipped my mind that John was a fan of Stormy's too.

'Well met young Deveroux. It has been a while, has it not? Well…don't just stand there. Hitch that nag to the back. She can help pushing us to Cambridge. You will ride with me, and we will catch up with the world.'

✪

We travelled North, along Ermine Street, and it was not an unpleasant journey. We continued into the early evening and stayed overnight at a coach house in Melbourn. It was after the sixth bell of the forenoon watch when the carriage arrived in Cambridge. I had ridden that last few miles on Strawberry, as John had work to complete and I needed to clear my head. It had been a heavy night. If John's head felt anything like mine, I truly can't begin to imagine how he could possibly read in a carriage that bounced every second moment…it would be beyond me.

John and I made arrangements to stay at the Eagle and Child tavern and, after a small luncheon, we made our way through the narrow streets to one of the smaller colleges of the great city. At the porter's lodge, we were escorted to the late Professor's rooms, which are located in Sherlock Court, off the main court - or quad as we of Pembroke College would have called it - and adjacent to the Old Library of St Catherine's College. Here we were shown up to a first floor apartment that looked out over the Master's lodge and garden. These where Witherspoon's rooms. They were neither small nor large but sort of alright-ish, if you follow.

The place itself was quite a mess, with academia strewn left, right, and centre. I took a gentle stroll around the apartment, picking up and studying objects that I found of interest.

A table map, drawn by Messrs Camden and Sons, a pearl-handled magnifying lens, a beautiful oriental chess set with pieces that I didn't even recognise. I picked up a red piece that had been displaced and looked at it with interest.

'The Mandarin. Sometimes called the Advisor or Minister. Beautiful, is it not? Made from the tusk of an elephant, I believe. It seems to have killed the black General, thus winning the game. I wonder how many elephants died to make this set?' John said with a sad, bitter smile.

The room also had a huge number of books on the Orient. It was then that I felt the gaze from a painting on the wall, as its eyes followed me across the room.

'It's all quite a mess.' I declared.

John was silent, but his eyes were as active as ever. He paid particular attention to the wine decanter and its glasses before turning to study the painting of Saint Sebastian. It was by an Italian artist, Cerrini, of whom I was not previously aware. It showed the Saint tied to a tree by the hands and feet. The bed chamber was off to the rear and its door opened to admit Richard Topcliffe, He was accompanied by a tall stranger. He closed the door quickly, yet still the odour of the dead drifted into the room.

'You are here at last,' Richard Topcliffe, the Inquisitor, stated. He gave a signal to the constables that were present, and they removed themselves. They looked pleased to be leaving the building.

'Excellent…we need a more esoteric view of this situation,' he said speaking to John,

'…and you, friend Thomas, you have a strange ability also.' He let his brownstained teeth show in what could have been a smile.

'This is my esteemed colleague, Doctor Niall Ó'Glacáin. We require his specialist medical knowledge in this investigation.'

Doctor Niall Ó'Glacáin was tall, thin man with long black hair, and whilst beardless, he carried the shadow of a few days' growth. His sparkling blue eyes twinkled behind a pair of glass lenses that balanced delicately on his nose. He had lost one of his front teeth and his tongue peeped at us from behind dark red lips. Although his smooth brogue, danced like music on my ear, it was somewhat difficult to decipher.

'Gentlemen.' He paused and looked at us in earnest, aware that he was not using our correct titles. He made no move to offer his hand.

'*A freethinker. A republican!*' I thought immediately.

'Prepare yourselves.' It was a clear statement.

'What you are about to witness has not been revealed to the public. It is indeed shocking. I have seen the rigours of war. I have seen flesh torn asunder. I have seen ritual killing. I have never seen anything like this.

'Please note that nothing in the room has been moved or removed.' He handed us each a face mask. They were shaped like a bird's head and had sweet smelling herbs inserted in the long beak-like nasal cone.

'You will need these masks. We call them plague masks. I had a score of them imported from the east. The body has begun the putrefaction process. Gases, fluids, and excreta are being expelled. It is not pleasant. However… that is not the most shocking fact… not the most shocking thing that you are about to observe.' He paused again, looking us deep in the eye.

'Vomit buckets have been placed by each wall,' he finished. He turned and walked back into the bedchamber.

25

The Body Adjacent to the Library

Sir Thomas Devereux; is with Doctor John Dee, when they meet Richard Topcliffe, the Inquisitor, and Doctor Niall Ó'Glacáin, the renowned medical surgeon, in the rooms of the late Professor Witherspoon, which are located in Sherlock Court, St Catherine's College, Cambridge. CB2 1RL

What occurred next is undoubtedly one of the strangest experiences of my short life. It ranks up there with the Battle of Hattin; indeed my whole Outremer adventure.

Later I found it hard to describe to others exactly what I saw. And believe me when I tell you that John had me recount the incident to him verbally, thrice, before committing my recollections to parchment. The circumstances were so strange that, as a writer, my imagination would find it impossible to conjure up their existence. And further, if I should achieve such a level of astonishing creativity, and expose my public to a correspondingly shocking story, I truly doubt if they would find it credible. More likely, it would be slammed by every critic, as a piece of puerile sensationalism, a staggering work of appalling fiction, and pure fantasy. And I doubt if anyone would wish to read pure fantasy. But here, as they say, is my account:

Witherspoon's body was suspended above the bed. It hung horizontally from a hook in the ceiling. It was attached to the hook by thick silken ropes. The ropes were double wrapped around his waist in a twining manner, first in one direction, and then in the other. Very neatly overlaid and rather like those that I have see on the mast of a sailing ship. Several strands were then twisted together, making the suspending strands into a thicker, stronger, cable-like strand.

Each of the bodies extremities were also bound. The arms were tied in similar twining fashion just above the wrist and the legs, likewise above the ankles, the strands again combining and each suspended separately from the same hook. One separate strand led to a substantial oval-harness type of fastening. This now hung loose at the front of the body, exactly where the head would have been.

I felt the vomit rise as my luncheon re-surfaced, and I headed for the nearest bucket. I rose and looked out of the small window. I could see a collection of students, and I'm sure some of the academic staff too, who were crowded into the small lane that led from the Main Court to the Master's Lodge. They peered at the building, jostling for a better position, a better view. I regarded their excited faces, wondering all the while what it is that makes people gawk so? I opened the window, breathing deeply, and allowing a small breeze to entered the room. It did not dissipate the stench at all, it just seemed to move it around, like a lazy concierge with a dirty mop.

Once I had regained control of my stomach, I gave Doctor Niall Ó'Glacáin all my attention. He

commenced his report in a matter of fact way. His
smooth brogue softening some vowels, and making
others sound somewhat harsher; or was that something in my mind?

✪

'As you will notice, gentlemen, the body is facing
the ceiling, expertly suspended, using something
that I believe is a far eastern rope technique. The
body is facing upwards, from our viewpoint. This
is no accident but a deliberate practice. It means
that yer man could watch the expressions and the
reactions of the Professor as they occurred. Cruelly,
it also means that the Professor could see each and
every procedure as it took place. He would anticipate
the insertion, the pain. Cruel…very cruel. Or is it
very professional?'
He paused for a moment, his eye moving to each
of us in turn, ensuring that this statement, like an
arrow, hit its mark.
'You will have noticed that the head has been removed. It has been carried away with the other body
parts. These are the trophies of the kill. Like the fox's
brush. I believe that the head was the last body item
to be removed. Yer man's primary aim seems to have
been to collect information. Information that the
Professor held. What information that could be is
beyond my scope…beyond my interest. Still, it's obvious to me that yer man did enjoy his *work*.' Again
he looked each of us directly in the eye.
'Yes, this is yer man's occupation alright. It is deliberate and it is organised work. This is more than
a mere occupation, it is yer man's vocation. And he
takes his time. He enjoys his work. He applies his

131

trade with pride. These cuts are detailed, accurate…
not mere hacking slashes. They are almost surgical
in their application. I believe that you are seeking a
professional man…a professional torturer. Someone
who has been trained in this…skill. And someone
who has done this work before…many times in my
opinion.'

'God's holy teeth…' said John, as he took his turn at
the buckets. I was surprised at this oath, as I knew
him to be an atheist, a man of science. He was not
absent long. His body shivered slightly as his hand
made a strange movement across his stomach and
he returned to the scene, losing no more than a moment.

'The fingers were removed first, one at a time,
starting with the right hand forefinger. It may even
have been removed in segments - that would inflict
the maximum pain, and prolong the…activity. I can't
be certain that they were removed in segments, as
the relevant body parts are missing…but it would be
logical to assume so,' Dr Ó'Glacáin reported matter of
factly.

'Once the excruciator ran out of fingers, he moved
on to the toes, where the same procedure was imple-
mented. Then, and here I speculate about the order
of removal you understand…yet I believe it would
be…would have more physiological impact, as we
call it…here yer man finally moved on to the balls,
and then next, the cock. I reckon this was more for
his own enjoyment and pleasure, than for the information required. Semen is present upon the professor's chest. Pure evil…nothing more. It is my belief
that any human would have given up his secrets
long before now, for surely the victims must have
endured this treatment for a hour or more. Still, it
would not kill him. Not for a long time. He would
have eventually, after hours, died from loss of blood.

Then the veins in his neck were cut.'

He removed the bird's head mask, headed for the door and into the main solar. We three followed him in a shocked silence. Once there, the Doctor concluded his report;

'The head was removed last - the final act. It's my opinion that yer man had gained whatever knowledge he had sought by then, if not long before the throat was severed or else he would have simply have started work on the teeth, and that would have left a lot of…debris…the appropriate flesh and tissue. No, he had achieved his purpose and was now probably getting bored.'

He removed his leather smock and stooped to wash his hands and then his face, before concluding;

'I am starving…shall we adjourn to the inn? I hear they do a nice bowl of trotters.'

The Eagle and Child, Cambridge

Sir Thomas Devereux; is with Doctor John Dee, Richard Topcliffe, the Inquisitor, and Doctor Niall Ó'Glacáin, the renowned medical surgeon, in the snug room of the Eagle and Child, Bene't Street, Cambridge CB2 3QN.

We made our way from St Kat's, passed St Benedict's Church, as we headed for the Eagle and Child, where an elderly woman showed us into the snug room and, once the pot boy had brought the beverages, we began to discuss the crime. Richard Topcliffe opened the discussion by asking Doctor Niall Ó'Glacáin to confirm his description of the excruciator.

'You believe we are looking for a professional man - a man with experience?' he asked. The doctor finished taking a gulp of dark beer, his Adam's apple sailing up and down his throat like the air bubble in the mercury of a weather barometer. He returned his tankard to the table with a small clatter before answering;

'For sure that's right. Yer man has experience. A skill set if you will. One that has taken time to learn. The rope technique. Unusual…if not darned right exotic. And the knife skill. An easy, steady nerve. As I said, the cuts are detailed, accurate, precise. Not an amateur…and not his first attempt.'

He drank again, finishing his tankard. John reached

for the bell pull and gave it a strong tug as the Doctor continued;

'The cuts, they are indeed surgical in nature. You seek a man that is trained for this work. It's as if the man attended a University of Torment, one like yer Dutch fellow…what is his name….the painter of hell?'

'Bosch, Hieronymus Bosch.' Stated John.

'Thats yer man…Hieronymus Bosch, even he could not have imagined this hell. This torment!' He said.

'But who could this torturer be?' I asked the ensemble.

'Let's draw up a list of potential suspects,' John said and he withdrew a notebook from his sleeve and started to write.

'His lover…this Garce Holdem- Downe,' Topcliffe immediately suggested, following his nose, like every policeman I had ever met. Doctor Ó'Glacáin finished his roast beef trencher and downed his tankard before he rose saying;

'Gentlemen, I will leave you to your deliberations. Who exactly yer man is…does not concern me. I deal only with the…method.' He moved quickly from the bench.

'Topcliffe - we will probably meet again soon. Doctor Dee…an honour to meet such an esteemed scholar. Please *do* call on me should you every need my assistance. And if you know of any Arabic books of medicine…I would be very obliged to be able to study them…If the Inquisitors would allow such.' He left the suggestion hanging, and glance at Topcliffe anxiously before turning to me.

'Sir Devereux…' He gave me a curt nod, and then exited the inn with long straight strides, his back as stiff as a board. John indicated that I should order another round of drinks, and as we waited for them to be delivered he recommended his thesis.

'There could well be a political motive.'

'How so?' Asked Topcliffe.

'The Treasure of The T'Ang. If the rumours are true, and Witherspoon had deciphered the code embedded with the vase that...' he looked at me, flashing a warning before his eyes quickly shot away again,

'... that this Mistress Miller had uncovered in Nottinghamshire.'

'Yorkshire!' I interjected and then felt his eye bore through to the back of my thick skull. I cursed my self for a fool.

'As our friend says...Yorkshire. Well, if he had deciphered the code... then...all the powers would make a bid...a secret treasure, a sum worth more than a prince's ransom? The greatest treasure in the world! Which nation would not be interested in acquiring such...it would create chaos...the power equilibrium would be unbalanced. The force of the great empires would be redistributed, its momentum shattered. And it would not just be the nations or the empires that would make such a move...a grab for this treasure. Each and every pretender, each would be king... for revolutions and revolts need funding too.

Even the Popes, the Pontiffs and Bishops of every church...each would fight for such a prize. It would mean the ultimate control of the whole world.'

He took a tankard from the serving boy and drank deeply. I looked at Topcliffe. His eyes had become as wide as the moon as the complexity of the situation began to dawn upon him.

'Who committed the act is one question; and one that you my dear Topcliffe will have to deal with. Who was behind the person, who commissioned the act, is another question entirely; for I doubt that this was any mean, jealous quarrel between lovers.'

Richard Topcliffe ran a hand over his stubbled chin.

He looked worried.

'International intrigue…that is beyond my scope. The acts of revolutionaries and plotters…I will report to my superiors. Common murderers are my bag…and I am charged to find a culprit. And before word and details of the crime can spread further abroad!'

He looked at us both slowly, as if to confirm that he had said his piece. Made his case.

'We will start the search for this Holdem- Downe. And any other of the Professor's lovers…whomever they may be. The rest I leave to you Doctor. You, Cecil and Walsingham; you are the council… and have the King's ear. I have my instructions. Find the culprit. The murderer. I will give you good afternoon…Sires.' He finished his beer and banged the tankard down with some aplomb, before turning and heading for the door. I watched him in silence.

'A morose fellow, what?' I breathed deeply and shuddered as if a shadow had fleetingly danced upon my grave.

'And not one I would like to cross,' I completed my sentence and waited for John to speak.

He said little for the next few moments and started scribbling in his note book. I knew him well enough not to interrupt and let him work while I nursed my dark beer.

27

Definitely, Maybe

Sir Thomas Devereux; is with Doctor John Dee in the snug room of the Eagle and Child, Bene't Street, Cambridge CB2 3QN.

We kept our silence for a good few moments. John continued to scratch his thoughts into his notebook. He paused every now and again, looking at me quizzically, before bending his head to his work once more. I sipped at my beer and looked about the room. Cambridge had changed little over the years. I had last been here less than a year ago, last autumn. Somehow I had managed to attend most of the Michaelmas term and was now, as a result, in danger of completing my degree. It had only take me eight years… not too shabby considering I had been to Europe with the Marshall, as his squire; and then onwards to Outremer, and Acre and finally back to Mighty Constantinople before returning, injured and demoralised.

It had been an adventure which had culminating in the fateful battle of Hattin and the death of my knight, Sir Rembald De Voczon.

'… Are you listening to me?' I heard John say as I surged out of my reverie.

'Ah…yes…but…no. I mean…' I stammered in my idiotic way.

'I was telling you something that I have not mentioned to the others. Something that we…we alone must keep secret. You can keep a secret can't you?'

'Well…no, not really. To be honest I have never tried…not a real secret anyway.' I said thinking of the secrets that I kept for Strix, and knowing that I had to fall back, resume my cover character quickly.

'Well you must keep this one. For if you fail…people will die. And I mean people that you know and love!' John scowled at me. He unquestionably had my attention now.

'Here is my list of potential culprits; those who may have committed this murder,' he said passing me a piece of paper.

'I have added a list of the potential villains responsible for this atrocity; for it may also be a plot against the king. This murder being *nought more than the opening act'*. As I have read in one of Marlowe's plays.'

'Actually, that was one of my lines. You know how these things work. The theatre owners want a rewrite or even a whole act; and they want it ready by tomorrow. So we meet up at The Magpie, off Grub Street, and work it together.'

'You know…we all chip in a bit. Swap work. Stick the thing together like a jigsaw, if you follow. Then Marlowe puts his name on it or sometimes an alias, and then divvies-up the advance later,' I answered as I took the paper from him and stated to glance at the list.

'I suggest that you commit this to memory and return it to me. Remember; *the walls have eyes; and sometimes they have ears too!*'

He added another name to the first list and gave

me that significant look again. And after a pause
added one last name to the second list. The lists read
thus;

*A List of Suspects in the case of the murder
of Professor Witherspoon.*

Topcliffe's Suspects

*Garce Holdem Downe
An unknown lover of Professor Wither-
spoon
A professional killer
A random stranger
Bonzo Barrington Browne*

*A list of potential Countries who could be
behind the instigation of the Murder of Professor Witherspoon;*

*Anjou
Frankia, and King Louis
Hibernia
Caledonia, and the Brothers Bruce [with
Hibernia?]
Espana*

And also;

*The Holy Roman Empire or a vassal state in
Germania, Hanover or Prussia
The Oriental Empire and the Princess Wu
The Colonies
Great Russia.
Lancaster, and the Lords Contrariants*

Other unknown but unhappy nobles;
Mortimer, Warwick, De Spencer, De Clare,
Badlesmere Etc.,
Isabella, The Queen
The Bloodline ~ Young Bess, Mary of Cale-
donia, The Grey Girl, Arabella Stuart
and others.
Edward II ~ The King

A list of people who are possibly in danger
for their lives, from the above, as a result of
this action;

Bonzo Barrington Browne
Garce Holdem Downe
Lady Yvette Waterton
Sir Thomas Devereux
Dr John Dee
Topcliffe
A professional killer

28

Watching The Detectives

Sir Thomas Devereux; is with Doctor John Dee in the snug room of the Eagle and Child, Bene't Street, Cambridge CB2 3QN.

I read the last list and gulped.

'You believe that these people, whoever they are, may try to kill us?' I ejaculated.

'It is not just a belief. I expect that it is likely. We are standing firmly in their path. We are endangering their stratagem. We have become a danger to their success,' John said labouring the point,

'…and so they will try to restrict our achievements. Eliminating us from the equation would be to their advantage. It is what I would do.' He gave me a quick flash of that hard stare; the one that he uses on people he dislikes, ensuring that I had comprehended his explanation. Then he continued;

'Now, let us remember the murder scene, and see what we can deduce. I hope, despite the gruesome spectacle, that you were able to keep your wits about you,' John said as he turned to a new page of his little black book.

'I will detail my observations, as I write, and you will tell me anything that you observed. Anything that I may have missed.' He stopped and looked around us before continuing;

'I cannot emphasis the fact that both our lives are

now in serious danger. And further, that anything we say here…is fatal…not only to us directly, but also to others. This investigation must be kept secret, silent, and as dark as the night.'

He began to scratch across the parchment. The carbon feather making a soft sound, quieter than the scratching of normal ink and feather; and that in itself gave the room an eerie aspect. I gulped at my beer and waited for the great man to speak.

'Tell me what you can remember of the details with regard to the position of the body,' he stated.

'Well, it was upward facing. And suspended about a cubit above the bed itself…by ropes, five strands in all, that stretched up to the hook in the ceiling. Above the bed. And it was aligned away from the door…so probably east,' I answered.

'Yes. The hook. Not a new hook, I noticed. This activity was not a new idea. Was it one of Witherspoon's passions? These adventures with ropes? And the height above the bed. Does that tell us that we maybe dealing with a smaller, rather than taller, man?' He asked.

'Yes. I'm not sure…definitely, maybe…I think so,' I said hesitantly.

'We should ask Bonzo. You realise that the higher the body is suspended, the more difficult it would be for a smaller man to do his…work?' John commented with authority.

'Now…the knotting - did you notice anything particular? Anything other than…as the good Doctor Niall called it…the *exotic* style?'

'Well…the knots that were used…they seemed similar to ones that I have seen used in the army.' I said.

'Excellent. That is good. It was a constrictor knot I believe. It is one of the most effective binding knots. But it is simple, and secure. A harsh knot though, and can be difficult to untie if over-tightened. It is made in a similar way to a clove hitch but with one end passed under the other, forming an overhand knot under a riding turn. This is not in common usage. As you say, they use it in some sections of the Army and the Navy. These knots must be an adaption that is used, apparently, in leisure bondage.' John said in his knowledgable way.

'I am curious as to how these exotic knots have been learned. Maybe someone who has been to the Orient? We will come back to this point.' He drew a star next to this passage in his notebook.

'Anything else?' He asked.

'Well yes. The candles. They were burnt down low. Nothing but the nubs were left,' I told him, and I blushed as John said; 'Outstanding, my dear fellow. Truly excellent. I did not notice that at all!'

John pulled the bell ring. The pot-boy arrived, and we order more beers. I noticed that a cat had sneaked into the room with him. It reminded me strangely of a cat I had know somewhere. It ignored me completely, like cats are oft want to do. I looked again and realised that it was a very different colour to the cat that I knew, lighter, almost a silver grey. It strolled around the room in an airy way before climbing onto the chair that Topcliffe had sat in, and then, curling its tail around its head, the way cats do, closed its eyes and prepared to take forty winks.

'I did notice though that the fellow had a small foot, with blood on his right sole and that he smoked a pipe,' John laughed and blew the foam from the top of his tankard.

'What!' I exclaimed, somewhat deflated that John had once again trumped my best trick.

'Ha…my point I think,' he said, smiling at me and winking.

'There was a half shoe mark on the sheet. You may

not have been able to see it from your side of the bed. But it was there. And I know that Topcliffe noticed it too. A right foot by its shape. But only the toe of the boot. So, the man must have stood in the blood that was pooling below the bed, as he climbed up to make adjustments to the ropes near the head harness.'

He grinned at me as I sat in amazement. I don't know why I was amazed. This man had been my private tutor when I was younger, after I had been expelled from King's School, Lincoln. You remember the incident with the Bishop and the bucket of water? And he had always been able to play this trick on me. He was without doubt one of the intelligentsia. Slowly he played his final card. He place a kerchief on the table and, unfolding it, revealed a very small pinch of tobacco.

'Lastly, there was this tobacco. It was spilt by the chair, the one near the far wall. It was only a pinch, and possibly not *our* mans' at all, but I think that it is likely. I think he stopped his task…for a while… and had a quiet smoke. Letting the pain, and the anticipation of more to come do its work. Letting the expectation do its work on poor Witherspoon. As the good Doctor said; 'A cruel man indeed.'

'But we can't sure that it is *our* mans' tobacco?' I said trying to regain a little ground.

'No, not sure…but it is a good guess. A strong probability. What's more it is a Turkish mix…not Virginian! And I noticed that Witherspoon smoked Virginian. He kept it in a carved box on his desk. Bonzo smokes, if not the same Virginian mix, then a very similar one. They may well visit the same tobacconist.'

He paused for a moment as he scribbled something else, then continued,

'So, as I say, a strong probability that it belonged to *our* man. I also think that there was a trace of opium powder mixed in with the tobacco. It had that smell, that taste. Once I have made a more complete test, I will be certain. That in itself could provide another clue to *our* man. Let us see what we have.'

He finished his writing and took another sip before starting to recap our observations.

'We are looking for a man. A man who is of smaller than average hight. He is right handed, and has blood on the sole of his right boot. He has a very special knowledge of anatomy; and also of knots and exotic rope work. These are skills that he has probably, if not certainly, learnt while he has been overseas. The East, if not the Far East. I would think the latter is almost definite. Especially if the opium is a habit. So...he is not a local, although he is probably from this island kingdom.'

Another sip, and a ponderous look;

'He is probably a reasonable good looking fellow, if maybe with a rough exterior. What is called 'ruggedly handsome' then. Handsome enough for Witherspoon to be attracted to him, and to allow him to enter his rooms, openly and unopposed, and to be tempted, lured, into a sexual encounter.'

He paused for a moment, rubbing the side of his head with his forefinger.

'Possibly the fellow has a glib tongue; for he convinced the Professor to be subjugated; And he is fit - indeed strong enough to overpower the man - so he has strength and is muscular. Strength enough to control his victim, whilst the bondage took place. Fitting a man's head into that harness would not be easy...not if the man resisted in any way.'

'What do you think he did with the...head...the body parts?' I asked reluctantly.

'Another good question my friend. What indeed. If we can locate those...trophies, then we are truly making progress, and yet...I feel that we will never will…still, we are closer than we were to finding *our* man.'

'Where would he have learnt such a roping style?' I asked, feeling a little overawed now.

'The Far East. Nippon or the Oriental empire. He may be a sailor. That would fit the profile. Perhaps a captured crusader. I know some such were sold into slavery along the Silk Road. Whichever, he also has great self-control, for he did not let the opium dominate him or he resisted it all together.' John said.

'So a man who is widely traveled.' I replied, taking a swift sup.

'There can be very few people who fit such a description.' I concluded, trying to sound intelligent.

'Indeed. And yet we are no closer to locating *this* man.' John said as he banged his tankard down on the table. The cat opened one bright blue eye and looked at him with a quiet disdain, before he yawned and stretched a rear leg. His tail swishing quickly, back and forth, then curling again around his head.

'And more importantly, I need to find out who his masters are. For this is just the excruciator, as the doctor called him, not the instigator. And the instigator has a plan…a program of events…ready to be unfurled.'

He leaned over and tugged on the bell-pull again. The door opened admitting Bonzo. We both looked at him in amazement. He stopped dead in his tracks. The pot-boy ran into his back. Once they had untangled themselves the pot-boy headed off to find more beer, and bring a extra tankard. Whilst Bonzo re-adjusted his immaculate ensemble.

'What?…Oh sorry, I was looking for you…Dev. I wondered…' his voice drifted away to nothing.

'Ah Barrington Browne,' said John kindly;

'Please be so good as to order my coach be made ready…will you? I must return to London…*instanta.*'

We said farewell, and John, finishing his tankard, departed for the metropolis but not before flashing me a look that told me to find out more about Bonzo's movements.

29

The Avenger

Strix; and Petrosinella, *the cat who lives with him, are in his solar at Number 7, Tweezer Alley, off Water Street, near the Temple Gardens, London WC3R 3LA.*

Petrosinella lay on the hearth rug, dosing fitfully in the mid-morning gloom. The word had spread, and she was in disgrace. Now, the magpies landed on the windowsill, delivered their messages but totally refused to enter my Tweezer Alley apartment. A mysterious chalk-like sigil had appeared on the wall outside. It was a declaration that this building was the scene of a murder. The place where poor Lorenzo had been fatally wounded, partially devoured, and it warned all concerned of the dangers involved in entering the property. I strongly suspect that the warning had been writ large, as it were, in dazzling yellow and white guano, by some up and coming street artist. I admired his work.

'Pjur, pjur, weer, weer. Queg, queg, queg,' said the bird as he landed. He demanded attention, like an angry passenger at the ferry docks. He did not introduce himself. A complete breach of etiquette.

'And so we have come to this.' I stated sadly;

'Not only will you not enter my home…but you fail in the basic courtisies.'

'Riik-rak-rak-rak, riik-rak-rak-rak.'

'Yes, I understand. And I have given the most abject apology to your Queen. I have apologised most profusely. Petrosinella has been punished, severely reprimanded, and she has suffered the most merciless admonition. I have confiscated her pilchards, and impounded her favourite cheese. Do you have a name, Sire?' I said, changing the subject.

'Pjur, pjur, riik-rak-rak-rak, wock a wock-wock a wock.' Said Mercutio, introducing himself formally, as magpies are wont to do.

'Riik-rak-rak-rak weer, weer. Queg, queg, queg,' he added, striding across the windowsill with a purpose.

'Ah…Mercutio the Avenger…the Slayer of Enemies.' I looked impressed, as I hid, deep within my beard, the small smile that grew on my lips. And with a bow of my head, I offered him my acknowledgement.

'Wock, wock, wock a wock. Pjur, pjur, queg, queg riik-rak-rak-rak. Pjur, pjur, weer, weer. weer, weer. Queg, queg, queg, queg.'

He explained that he was the Wreath Layer at the death ritual of the departed Lorenzo.

'I am Strix. A friend to your Tiding, and to all magpies.' I said formally.

'And how can I help…such a noble warrior today?' I said, using a ladle to lay on the syrup with a surplus. Mercutio hopped onto my arm and allowed me to remove the small piece of parchment attached to his leg. It was cached in a leather pouch affair that had obviously been handmade for the purpose.

'A letter from your Mistress,' I remarked, as I removed the secret communication.

Mercutio leaped in to the air, circling the room once. He crapped on Petrosinella's head, as he flew over her. A direct hit. Petrosinella screeched; a cry of despair, before she scrambled to take cover under the low bed, that rested in the corner of the chamber.

I read the letter;

I bent to fashion a response. However, when I looked around, Mercutio had flown, leaving a distinctive trail of guano across the hearth rug;

'Pjur-rak.' It spelt.

'Death to all cats.' I read.

'See what trouble you have caused now!' I remarked to the trembling Petrosinella.

I spent the rest of the morning hastily implementing plans that had been long in their preparation. Pigeons flew from my loft on every bell. The Mistress of Darkness was right. Time *was* of the essence. How had this happened? Did the King know? What about

the Pope? Gods…the Pope has spies everywhere…
how could he not know? This really could be a cataclysmic problem for the movement. The Boy…
were we fully prepared? We should not panic. It is
the impulsivity of youth - they simple can not abide
waiting,' I told Petrosinella, who peeked at me from
under the bed and cowered every time a bird landed
upon our windowsill.

30

About A Boy

Strix; is in his solar at Number 7, Tweezer Alley, off Water Street, near the Temple Gardens, London WC3R 3LA.

The Boy was a development that hadn't been totally unforeseen…you see there was a myth. Every child knew the story. It had circulated for a millennia or more but for the myth to become reality…was, well, unanticipated. I would need to consult with Dr Dee. He knew more about the prophecy than anyone. Had he got his theory wrong? And consulting him… that, in itself, was going to be an altogether different problem, and a dangerous one…far more complex than anything I had yet attempted. I summoned up my nerve, found it lacking in stamina and so made myself a hot toddy to inject some backbone. Once the warm feeling had spread through my stomach, I pulled the shutters close. The sun was still passing high across the sky and the noon-tide bell had rung only a few moments ago. Outside it was a bright day, if chilly in the shadows. I pulled the window hangings together, and thus the chamber fell into a semi-darkness.

'Ambience. It's all about the ambience.' I told Petrosinella nervously. Soon the candles were flickering and incense filled the chamber with a heady scent of patchouli oil. Small bells chimed together, as the draughts in the room caught them. I starred intensely at my crystal, my eyes never blinking. I could feel the light-headed sensation starting to grow. I seemed to sink further and further into the swirling beams of light as they danced within the crystal. Then they began dancing within my mind, and my mind reached out for them, gently probing the space between the air and, well…time itself. Touching, feeling, sifting. Concentrating on the image of John Dee. Willing him to respond to me.

At first it was the very merest of suggestions. A single glimpse, on the edge of my vision, as if it were just behind me. Just on the border of my eyeline. Slowly, the sense of his library swam into my mind, quietly creeping up on me like a silhouette emerging from the darkest of shadows. It started to grow there, still on the very edge on my vision. Not quite a solid mass, and yet, at the same time, giving the impression that it was.

Gradually he faded into my vision. He was bent over his own scrivening ball. This was a new sensation for me. John didn't seem to know that I was here?…there? Whichever… He ignored me, continuing with his own work, as if he was contacting someone else. Could he be contact someone else? Could he *be* in contact with someone else? If so, would I be able to hear who he had contacted? Would he be able to hear me? The questions rushed through my mind, which whirled like a weathercock in a storm. I pushed them back, keeping my focus gently on the light as it twisted and flowed, ebbed, and fluxed between us…just one more moment, and then…we would have contact.

'…You will have to let him go…you know that…it is the simple truth…we have had this conversation many times my dear, but now…the sands of time are spent, and Cronus has swung his scythe.' He spoke to another. A hidden contact.

'Don't you know it's rude to eavesdrop!'

The Voice! It screamed at me. And *she* was using The Voice! My mind shuddered, as if a thunderbolt had been directed straight between my eyes. I reeled backwards, falling off my stool. My head throbbed, as if I had been punched in the brain, and my eyes stung as they started to swell and the bruising grew.

'That is for Lorenzo!'

The connection was broken.

31

The Blue Oyster Cult

Sir Thomas Devereux; is with his friend and companion of yesteryear, Bonzo Barrington~Browne. They are seated in the snug room of the Eagle and Child, Bene't Street, Cambridge CB2 3QN.

'W-w-was it something that I said?' asked Bonzo, as John Dee left the building to return to London. Bonzo has a slight stammer which always becomes more pronounced when he becomes nervous.

'I doubt it, Bonzo. John has a lot on his mind. This intrigue is of paramount importance to him. Don't give it another thought.' I told him, not mentioning the fact that Bonzo was on John's list of possible suspects in the murder of Professor Witherspoon.

I had not seen Bonzo since we had met, by chance, in the Nellie Dean that last time. The time I was there to meet Strix. And had not spoken at any length with him since the Messrs Camden's party. And so I was in the dark as to his involvement with Witherspoon. Of course I knew that he wasn't the murderer but what had happened since that evening? The evening when they left the party together?

And of course, I knew that they both worked at St Catherine's College, and so must have met often. I also wondered where my vase was and what exactly had happened to it?

'I-I'm sorry about the other day.' Said Bonzo picking up my thoughts almost telepathically, like close friends often do.

'S -Strix I mean…in the Nellie Dean…d-don't you know. I was in such a flap, and I wasn't really sure what I was to say in front of you. Strix has since cleared everything though. He let me know that we're on the same side, as it were. He has suggested that I should cooperate with you…let you know anything that may be relevant…that may be of help you, as it were, with reference to old Witherspoon.'

His face flushed a pinkish red and reminded me of the map of the world, highlighting the empire as it radiated outwards from England in all directions. Bonzo turning up here, today, had not really surprised me. After all he was obviously involved, immersed in the situation, and so I started talking generally, just to break the awkward silence that was growing between us, yet still seriously aware that I needed to be careful of what I said to him. After all, I was working for two masters now; Strix and John Dee both. Still, Bonzo did have information that Strix may have known first…and that John would want to…need to know, if you follow me.

'I bet they had a good time removing old Witherspoon's collection of bondage accoutrements.' Bonzo announced, again synchronising his thoughts with mine.

'Yes, Topcliffe, the Inquisitor, believes that it maybe a crime of passion, as the Messrs Camden suggested, after all?' I picked up the cat that had been fussing around my legs and started stroking him. He purred softly, his paws kneading my leg. And all the time I wondered;

'How much does Bonzo really know?'

'Were you aware of anything unusual Bonzo?'

'No, nothing out of the ordinary. However everything about Witherspoon was kind of unusual. You know…eccentric? Not that I would know what exactly you would be looking for...No, nothing strange,' he replied. And I suddenly got the feeling that he was trying to find out what I knew. And that was strange in its self.

'Tell me what happened the night that you and Old Wither's left the Camden's party early, would you Bonzo?' I asked him, approaching the awkward subject head on. Bonzo turned a brighter red than ever, almost approaching vermillion and started to stammer again.

'W-well, you know the Professor was into Sinology.'

'He was into one or two other leisure activities too,' I couldn't help but insert. Quite wrong of me I know, but one simply must smile at life's opportunities as one passes through the duller moments.

'And he wanted to see that vase, the one Yvette gave to you,' Bonzo continued, quite correctly ignoring my facetious remark.

'So, I toddled off with him. Showed him the vase in your rooms, and then about ten minutes later went back to the party.' Bonzo looked embarrassed and stammered on...

'W-w-well, you know his reputation, I-I suppose?' I nodded and Bonzo, seeming somewhat relieved, continued his tale.

'I thought that I had better not encourage him, so I decided to decline the offer of supper at his club, and instead gave him the vase to inspect.'

I just smiled to myself and thought;

'*I bet he was disappointed.*'

'Anyway, after a while, the professor seemed to forget that I was there at all, and he started to talk to himself. He was mumbling on about the vase.

'Well after a minute or two he was almost ranting. He became *so* excited. To put the thing in a nutshell, he was simply thrilled. He said that the vase was most unusual in its design. In so much that most of

the symbolisms employed within the design were of
an age far earlier than that of the pattern, in which
they were encompassed. As if they were hidden.
They were apparently, and he presumed here that I
knew all about the T'Ang dynasty, not at all contem-
porary with the main story of the vase. He believed
that the vase could be at least three hundred years
older, later…earlier…before…yes, before the T'Ang.'
Bonzo sounded confused and paused for breath;

'Before. Earlier than originally thought. He called it
a Memorial Vase. He said that they very rarely falsi-
fied the facts, but often obscured the true meanings
of them. What I mean is that there seemed to be a
sub-text to the general story.

Well, at least that's what I thought the old sod
meant. The professor wanted to study the vase
further, and asked if I would leave it with him for a
while, so that he could spend some time researching
the symbolism. And I thought that you wouldn't
mind, so…' He looked at me shyly; to see if I would be
annoyed at this. I shook my head indicating it was of
no matter. But I was annoyed. Very annoyed indeed.
After all, Yvette had given me that vase.

'He was particularly interested in one symbol,
which he said defined an oyster, or more correctly…'
Here he paused to get the precise wording;

'The pearl within the oyster. It was blue symbol. I
can't forget how really excited he had become about
it. He said that there was some kind of cult that
worshipped this oyster symbol.' He paused again and
took a sip.

'…Sounded like tosh to me. Anyway he went on
and on about it. Quite lucky really, since it seems to
have distracted him from other pleasures that I fear
he may have had on his mind when I first entered
your rooms…' His voice trailed off and he looked at
me sideways.

'You do know that...that fellow Anatole was crashed out in a drunken heap on your bed don't you?' he finished, trying to change the subject to something more palatable.

'Most interesting, young Bonzo.' I said, steepling my hands and trying to sound like John.

'What happened then?'

'Well, about a week later - no, three or four days or so...I got a message asking me to attend one of the lectures that Witherspoon was giving. Quite mysterious really, but since he was one of my colleagues...

Anyway, I popped along to the hall and was pleasantly surprised to find that the subject of his lecture was the vase. Didn't he invite you? No. Well, that's the juice of the story.'

'So what did he say about the vase?' I asked. I was really becoming intrigued and little white clouds were replacing the grey ones that normally float along in my mind's eye, and small, very small, rays of sunlight were beginning to appear. Rather like one of those paintings by the great masters. Poussin, or some such.

'Well, it turns out, the professor had explained, that the tradition of painting stories on to vases began during the T'Ang dynasty, with the use of symbolism to tell the story, you understand? This practise had been well known for some time. However, the Professor had been researching the fact that certain of these well-known vase stories included a secret subtext. And that these subtexts had been painted into the existing patterns and designs.'

'Like a code?' I asked him excitedly, all the while thinking that this was just up Strix's street. John's too for that matter.

'Yes. Witherspoon said that the vases did not exactly falsify the facts, the gist of the story but truly made them much more obscure.' He paused and slurped again. I joined him.

'It seems that was done by using the wrong symbols, older symbols, symbols from the previous dynasty. Symbols that are very similar to the traditional ones, and yet incorporated subtle differences, very subtle differences it seems. Differences, which would appear almost as if they were small errors… that is if anyone should happen to notice them at all, underneath all that din sum.'

We both looked around the room and without saying a thing decided that we should speak more softly. Bonzo continued his story;

'Anyway, it seems that these slightly altered or different symbols were indeed an ancient secret code, and that they had been placed within the existing pattern in order to conceal the message's true meaning. The professor had managed to decipher part of the message, and he did say that he was very pleased with the results and that the Sinologist Society was going to publish his theory in their next quarterly. That was all there was to it really.' Bonzo concluded.

'Did Witherspoon explain to you what the story was about?' I asked him.

'Well no, not really. After the lecture, I met with the Professor and he asked if he could possibly take me to dinner. Of course I declined, and made a hasty retreat - a bit like we did at the Fall of Acre.'

'Please Bonzo, don't mention the Holy Lands, the years are passing but the wounds are still fresh. The ransom hurt mother's pocket deeply, and she will never let me forget it.

And Bannockburn was even worse. If that is possible. Edward, His Grace, simply ran away leaving us to fight a hastily organised withdrawal over that damned marsh. Though it seems to me, if I remember correctly, that you managed to duck out of that one somehow,' I told him with a nasty tone in my voice and a meaningful look, as I rubbed my thigh.

'Yes, Bannockburn, a bad business…the old teaching wheeze got me out of that one.' Bonzo said looking sheepish, if someone with a face like an angel fish can look sheepish.

'A most intriguing story. Shall we make our way to a chop house?' I asked. The cat gave me a flash of his blue eyes, as I let him leap to the floor and he followed us out of the room.

In the dark passage that ran behind the snug, the hostess rubbed her ear. Keeping it pressed to the small hole in the wall for the last two hours had been painful. Still, her master would be very pleased with this news. And hopefully generous too.

32

Assassins Creed

Sir Thomas Devereux; is with his friend and companion of yesteryear, Bonzo Barrington Browne. They are leaving the Eagle and Child, Bene't Street, Cambridge CB2 3QN.

Cambridge was a place that Bonzo and I knew well. We had both been sentenced to longish terms of incarceration in the establishment here since we were gangly youths in our early teens. Bonzo being seriously more gangly than anyone else you have ever seen. The objective was for us to obtain an education of sorts. In fact Bonzo was still here and I had been finishing-off, as they say, only last year. I *had* received an education of a kind.

Probably not the one that Father had paid for, and one that was somewhat curtailed by my rustication - you remember that incident with the Bishop and the bucket of water. Still, it did explain some of my life's endeavours thus far.

Bonzo had done rather better than me. That is why he is now a Professor of something. Aristotelian Ethics…that's the baby, I remember now. Mind you, how someone like Bonzo can be expected to lecture to others on the subject of Moral Philosophy is quite beyond me. I seem to recall that he spent most of his time at the University drinking, gambling, and chasing ladies of dubious character. And I should know, for I was right there with him, neck and neck at the finish, if you catch my drift. The two of us being the nearest to bosom pals as could be.

As we made our way past St Bene't's Church, heading to the Eagle and Child, something very strange happened. At the end of a small tunnel-like passage, formed by the overhang of the upper stories of the houses there, a small man could be seen scurrying towards us. His body, though facing us, seemed to be moving in a sideways, crab-like motion. He was hooded, and kept his face tilted down, so that we could not see his features clearly at all. Then, just as he drew near to us, he swung his right hand up quickly. I saw the dagger's blade glint in the night.

Before either of us could make a move to draw our blades there was a whooshing sound, followed by a dull squashy thud, and the man stopped in his tracks. He slowly sagged at the knees and began to fall backwards. He lay sprawled on the cobbles, releasing one soft groan, and then he was gone. He was as dead as a doornail. Blood was bubbling from a wound on his forehead. A small pebble was embedded there.

'It looks like an island, set in a ruby sea.' Said Bonzo.

'No, the yoke of a fried egg as painted by an artist with tritanopia or one who has exceedingly strong herbs in his pipe.' I stated

As we discussed these alternatives, I realised that the assassin looked familiar; those dark sullen eyes, now permanently morose. That heavy brown moustache still matted and dull. Those short, stubby, dirty fingers, that gripped a bejewelled dagger.

The stiletto dagger lay in his hand which had fallen across his chest. It was a dagger I had seen before. Even from where I stood, I could see that it was a lethal stiletto dagger, made of beautifully folded steel, with an ebony handle, that held a small jewel which glistened, blood red.

He lay silent, sullen, moody, and more unresponsive than I had ever seen him before. A condition that now would never improve.

'Dev…I think that it is your roommate!' exclaimed Bonzo in shock.

'Yes, Sir Anatole de Sourisblanche,' I replied studding the corpse.

'It appears that he is now mortally delinquent with regards to the rent arrears.' I concluded. I looked around - even though it was still early in the evening there was no one in sight.

'Bonzo, we should scarper…sharpish, before the Dibble arrive.'

I made a quick searched of the body foraging for clues. All I found was a letter, a folded newssheet, and a small bag of golden doubloons.

'How curious;' I thought as I trousered them quickly and collected the dagger from his lifeless hand. My mind was reeling as the thoughts pounded it, like waves pounding on a rock headland.

'Mother's dagger! Mother's dagger? What could that mean? Had she tried to have me murdered? Assassinated?

I heard the soft shuffle of well-padded feet behind me. I turned around quickly, expecting a new attack. I could see nothing there at all. Just a dark gloom that filled the alley. A hard shadow emerged from the gloom. A small figure emerged from the shadow. He stood in front of us. He held a catapult firmly in his left hand. He stood for a moment, silent, then he took a small, awkward bow.

'Here's Nosher.'

33

Judy Teen

Manus O'Heron; *the Special Correspondent for the news-sheet 'The Tears of Hermes' is at the scribing desk marked 'Press.' He is making copious notes. The Judge, Doctor Joseph Sopenhiemer, is presiding at the trial of a multiple murder. The accused, Sweet Lightborne, stands facing his accusers. PC 31, an Officer of the Watch, is about to give his evidence. Kit Marlowe, the eminent playwright, is sitting in the bar, off the main chamber and supping a light beer. What seems like the entire population of Canterbury are expectantly gathered to celebrate the proceedings. The whole occupy the Old Yew Tree Inn, 32 Westbere Lane, Westbere, Canterbury, CT2 0HH*

'This court is now in session! The Honourable Dr Joseph Sopenhiemer, M'Lord presiding,' said the court usher loudly as Dr Joseph Sopenhiemer, M'Lord entered the chamber and took his seat.

'Give your evidence, constable,' demanded Soapy. I noticed that Kit Marlowe, the famous playwright, slipped into the room and stood behind the crowd to the rear. I studied them all, in my role as special correspondent from the *Tears of Hermes* and, taking the feather from my hat, with inkstained fingers I started to write;

'*Standing before the court confidently, in his dress uniform, showing the watch insignia and a five year service ribbon, the constable, commenced his statement…'*

★

P.C. Thirty and one said;

'We caught a dirty one…M'Lord. A villain, going by the name of Sweet Lightborne. He was involved in an assault, a violent assault, on three individuals, resulting in the murder of two…and grievous injuries to the woman, who may still die from her wounds. The incident occurred at the Old Neptune, on Marine Terrace, next to the Island Wall, in Whitstable, CT5 1EJ, late on the night of Friday last. About five bells of the First Watch. Two days ago, Your Worshipfulness.' He coughed and adjusted his gambeson.

'Three people?' enquired Soapy.

'Yes, Your Honour. A doxy called Judy Teen, renowned *'Queen of the Night'*, her minder, Max Silverhammer, and a sailor; known locally as Happy Jacques…from the provinces he was. La Rochelle, I believe.'

'And this man dispatched all three, you say?'

'Yes, Your Honour. He attacked the young woman first, cutting her on the face, arms and belly, before killing Max Silverhammer with a stab wound in the gizzard. The sailor he cut from ear to ear,' the constable drew his thumb across his neck, 'leaving him with a second smile.'

'What say you Lightborne?' Soapy asked the prisoner, peering at him over a large pair of eye lenses. The accused replied in a sing-song voice with a cockney accent;

★

'Judy Teen,
Was Queen of the Scene,
She was always around,

Helter Shelter,
Nowhere to shelter,
Was to be found,

Tutti Frutti,
No sleeping beauty,
But sound as a pound,

Hanky Panky,
She tried to spank me,
She was renowned,

Heebie Jeebies,
She gonna leave me,
Tortured and bound,

Ruff and Tumble,
You mustn't grumble,
On your head, you'll be crowned,

Handy Dandy,
She gonna hang me,
Murdered and drowned,

Judy Teen,
Was Queen of the Scene,
No longer around,'

The crowd buzzed in awed appreciation of his rhyming skills. Some even clapped. A girl in the front threw a kerchief at him.

Bang! Bang!

Soapy's gavel came down upon the wooden table. My quill scratched across the parchment. Marlowe was looking bored as he finished his beer. Lightborne change the tempo of his performance.

> '*The Moxy-Doxy,*
> *Tried to fox me,*
> *Tried to grab my poke,*
> *Hard earned that was,*
> *The profit from the Prof.,*
> *Wergeld. Moi Oro. My Gold.*
>
> *A purse of gold,*
> *For a man who's bold.*
> *A man who knows his work,*
> *Wages of sin,*
> *Expert in pain,*
> *Learned from the heathen Turk.*'

Lightborne's rhyming speech maintained its sing-song tone, and he told his story easily. All the while his eyes gleamed intensely as they traveled across the room. They finally came to rest on Marlowe. He seemed pleased that a noted playwright should be in attendance. He nodded towards him in recognition. Noticing this, as all good correspondents would, I scribbled faster than ever, ink splashing, yet again, across my long dark cloak.

'For I am but an actor,
The merest, meekest cats-paw,
Upon the playwright's stage,
Torture, murder, mayhem
Whenever you demand them
In blood, I earn my wage.'

He said quizzically to the crowd before returning to his story.

'Push a needle fine,
Through a neck, so divine,
And watched her life ease by.
A small ribbon of red,
Trickles, and she's dead,
Her life is over, it has run dry.'

'And the others?' asked the judge.

'Easy-peasy,
Like lemon Squeese-y,
I've killed many a man,
Enjoy your work,
No time to shirk,
Death; I lend a helping hand.'

I wrote on:

'The accused paused, and a smile spread across his face at the memory. He looked like a small, dark eyed child, remembering a kindness from his Grand-Mere.'

'The big man was strong,
 Max Silverhammer,
A street fighter, of honour and re-
nown,
I made him wriggle,
I made him jiggle,
My sweet blade did lay him down.'

'The sailor was small,
But strong as a bull,
He gave me a right vicious kick,
I drew him a smile,
Crimson is style,
And left him…lickety split.'

'And then came the Dibble,
Fast as a fiddle,
Took me from behind,
With billy stick,
Hit me, bosh…damned quick,
Bonce bruised, me battered, and
entwined.'

★

Lightborne grumbled as he finished, and the crowded murmured their agreement;
'Such ungentlemanly conduct, damned right unsporting, and exceedingly unfair. Always the way these foreigners and the dibble, well…it should be banned. A fights, all right, if it's a fair fight.'
As the murmuring spread Lightborne's smile turned into a grin, and he winked at the woman who

had thrown the kerchief.

Dr Sopenhiemer banged his gavel again before stating;

'Yes, indeed. It seems as if your work is complete. What I wish to know is who you have been working for? Who is your employer? For there would appear to be far more behind this occurrence that meets the eye!'

The usher brought the black cap and draped it over the judge's wig. Then, The Honourable Dr Joseph Sopenhiemer, M'Lord, made his pronouncement. His judgement. The sentence.

'You confess that you are a torturer, a trained killer, and a murderer. And that this is your occupation - the work that you have chosen to do. Your career. And what is more, one that give you a lucrative income. Although, in this particular case, not one from which you shall profit.' He paused and gave a hard stare to the accused.

'And so I sentence you to the death penalty. The High Inquisitors will spend some time with you. That, I believe, will be a conversation worth the hearing. But first you will rot in our excellent oubliette. That will give you time to contemplate your life, your deeds. Then, when we are ready, you will be hanged by the neck.

'Three times you will hang. Once for each murder until finally dead. Your body will be caged and hung outside our city. Food for the carrion birds. A warning that the King's law rules here.'

The gavel banged again.

'Officer of The Watch take him to the Whitehouse

Cage.'

'Manus O'Heron, special correspondent for *The Tears of Hermes* your honour; What of the Doxy - did she die?' I shouted the question to the judge but gained no answer.

At the back of the chamber Kit Marlowe watched the proceedings. He looked at the judge and nodded his head in agreement with the sentence. The murderer looked him straight in the eye.

'Maybe you'll put me in a play of yours, eh?' suggested Lightborne, as the dibble began roughly handling him out of the chamber. The Black Maria stood waiting. As they moved towards it, he dropped back into his sing-song voice and sang over his shoulder.

> *'Oh pretty, pretty boy…*
> *So full of life, so full of joy…*
> *You play a dangerous game?*
> *In the Cage I will wait,*
> *'till you open up the gate,*
> *For yours I am… to reclaim.'*

✪

Marlowe gave no answer. I watched as he ran his finger down the side of his nose and followed him as he exited the inn. He headed down the street, taking long strides, as he made for his father's workshop.

'Manus O'Heron, special Correspondent for *The Tears of Hermes*, Sire…Any comments on the judgement? The condemned seemed to be aware of you. Do you know him? Mess'r Marlowe - do you have any comments?'

I chased after him, through the small streets of

Canterbury, my quill once again perched in my hat, with scraps of parchment bulging from the recesses of my cloak. The questions bubbled upon my lips and headlines floated through my mind;

'Canterbury Cut-Throat [28] Slays Three'

34

Not Your Gods

Lady Yvette Waterton; is at The Watermill, Axholme, which nestles in the bottom corner of Yorkshire, on the borders of Nottinghamshire and Lincolnshire, in that part of the Kingdom known as North of the Gap. DN10 6 HN

'Thank you for your kindness Mistress Yvette, the Gods will bless you,' said the Boy when I re-entered the room. He was eating his cheese with zeal, as if he had not eaten for a week.

'Well that doesn't sound too heretical now does it?' I replied,

'How long have you been on the road for, Boy?' I asked him.

'Oh, only a week. I have travelled from Rievaulx. It's not that far, but I got a little lost and I ended up too near to the forest, and had to double back upon myself. I nearly got feathered there. It is very wild country, and some men were out hunting for deer.'

'Yes, these days there are many wild men loose in the countryside. These are desperate times for many. And a desperate man has nothing left to lose. I help as many as I can, but these Black Laws…damn this King and his harrying,' I continued.

'And when do you have to be at the Abbey?'

'Well, when I get there, then that is when I will need to be there,' the Boy replied with an easy smile.

'I do not know if they will take me, or even what I will do there, nor if I will be allowed to take my vows. I'm not even sure where Revesby is,' he said with a shrug of his shoulders.

'Oh, maybe I can help you.' I told him,

'I know someone who will guide you to Revesby. It may take a few days for him to get here, but he is the best guide in the land. They say he has Faerie bloode. I will make a bargain with you Boy - if you can help me with the vegetable garden and some of the mill work, I will put you up and feed you for a few days, and then, I will be able to supply travel, food, and arrange an escort for you to the abbey. It is not easy to find, you know. It lays across the Lincolnshire marshes. How does that sound to you?' I asked him.

'It would be nice to have a roof for a night or two, and warm food does sound divine. I bless you for your kindness, Mistress Yvette. The Gods will smile upon you, and bless you.'

'Yes, as maybe…but I think…not your gods.'

35

Love Labour's Lost

Dr John Dee; is in his solar at River House, which stands in large grounds between the High Street and the river Thames, next to the church of St Mary the Virgin, in Mortlake, London, SW14 8JA

'And why should I?' She crossed her arms and scowled at me.

'He is needed. I have work for him to do. He is a prime element in the great game.'

'You and your great game! What care I for your great game? Am I not important too? What of my dreams, my desires, my feelings…?'

The tears came in a stream. Her eyes were wild, she was near to losing total control. And nobody really understands what happen when magic and emotions become mixed. It could lead to a very explosive situation. A mad witch is a very dangerous thing indeed.

'So that you can gift him to this princess of yours? A poor play mare. I could wipe her from this world and the next with just one glance!'

'Yes. Indeed, and still you won't. And why? Because you too know that she is also of prime importance to our movement. The Princess to our Knight. The great game moves across the chess board and without her in power, how will we achieve the thing that we both desire? What if the Pope was to make that

dreadful Caledonian girl Queen? What then?' I realised that I was sweating and slowed my pace, changing my tone and letting a calming influence seep into
my words.

'It is hard for you. I know but you too know that...
sometimes things are bigger than the individual.
Bigger than one person. You know that we must all
make sacrifices,' I released a long breath and curved
my fingers, palms upwards, and spoke softly, letting
my voice flow smoothly into the room.

'Of course you are important. And I realise that
what I ask of you is not...an easy thing but...we...
you must envisage the whole, the complete body,
the complexity of the entire ensemble, including the
things that affects the whole...not just one single
part of it.

Like the chess game, we must think two moves
ahead. You will have to let him go. You know that. It
is the simple truth. We have had this conversation
many times my dear, but now...the sands of time are
spent, and Cronus has swung his scythe.'

'Don't you know it's rude to eavesdrop!' She
screamed and thunder roared in my ears.

I suddenly felt another presence. The connection
broke immediately.

'Wha...' I managed to stumble the sound out.

'Strix! Did you have Strix eavesdrop on our conversation? You dirty old man. How dare you!'

'Strix. Who is Strix?' I declared, now totally confused.

'You have the barefaced cheek to tell me that you
don't know him!' she was screaming now.

'You are despicable. Simply...' She began to cry
again.

'My dear, I had no knowledge of this Strix, nor of
any who knows him. I had no idea that he was there.
No idea that he was able to contemplate...eavesdrop-

ping upon us…or upon anyone…quite an interesting idea though. I suppose it could be done, if…'

'Don't you try to mollycoddle me!' she roared and her vision grew within my sight.

I watched as she crossed her hands upon her chest and smoke eddied around her as she faded from my view.

'I hope I never see you again. In this world or the next…you devious little man!'

Still her eyes scowled at me through the ether, and my scrivening ball rose alarmingly from my table and hovered for a moment, before it hurled itself at the fire place. It smashed in to a thousand pieces, which fell upon the hearth rug, and looked, for all the world, like a new map of the cosmos.

'Oh but you will…and that is something that I shudder to contemplate.' I said to myself.

36

Topcliffe Goes To Nottingham

Richard Topcliffe; *The Inquisitor has been summoned to appear before the King, Edward of Caernarfon and the royal court, who have congregated for the feast of Lammas, which they celebrate at Nottingham Castle, NG1 6EL.*

The court was buzzing. A low hum that turned into a silence as I passed the assembled nobles. They watched me carefully with an open dislike, one that they did not even attempt to conceal. I ignored them the best that I could.

I passed a tall thin man dressed all in black, as I found myself a place near the great widow and I stood alone looking down from the massive hill. The lowland area stretched out before me. Here the docks stretch from the canal across the land to the mighty river Trent, which in turn rolled, fat and lazy, through the middle kingdom and out to the Great North Sea.

It was a grey day. Still, so far this week, the rain had held off and now the flooding had started to recede. It had left destruction behind. The land was covered in a thick mud and detritus. The weather was another problem that the Gods were giving this young king. And one he could do little about. The rain was ruining the crops and flooding many of the lowland areas. More and more storms were occurring and they seemed to be becoming ever more furious. Yes, the Gods were giving this young king a hard reign.

The court had other problems too; Old Gaul, Hibernia, The Oriental Empire, The Opium Wars and civil unrest North of the Gap.

However, I had other things on my mind. This murder in Cambridge needed to be brought to a conclusion. The High Inquisitor had left me in no doubt about that. Nor - if I was to fail - who would be held responsible. Then too there was the problem of the Freethinkers, the Pamphleteers, the Witches, and those rumours of The Boy. That was only a myth though…wasn't it?

✪

'Mister Topcliffe…' His Grace looked at me for a long time. He had a curious half smile on his face. His favourite Piers Gaveston sat at his feet, strumming on a mandolin.

'… You are related to the old Baron Burgh, The Tyrant of Gainsborough, I believe?' the King asked, not taking his eyes from me.

'You have lands but no title…as yet?' he concluded.

'Yes Sire, he was my deceased mother's father. My Grandsire, he raised me up. After my parents died. But he also declared me illegitimate, as he had disinherited my mother and refused to recognise the legitimacy of her wedding, Your Grace.'

'Yet he sent you to the Lincoln School did he not?'

'Yes, Your Grace.'

'And now you are one of my Inquisitors. Tell me… do you like your work?'

'I find it interesting. A challenge. Your Grace.'

'If you are successful Topcliffe we may be able to

revisit this matter of your legitimacy and that of course would re-establish your position, would it not?'

I nodded my agreement and bowed low.

'Yes indeed…you are very gracious, Your Grace.' I said realising that it was a stupid thing to say. Gracious Grace! Gaveston laughed at my embarrassment and spoke for the first time.

'I like this man Edward. *Il est un rougue honnête est-il pas?* How you say; An honest rogue. And we need a few rogues in this world do we not?'

Edward joined him in the joke and I blushed as they laughed at the jest.

'So…Topcliffe. Tell me of this Cambridge affair. I hear it is quite sensational.'

✪

' … And those are the details You Grace. I have never seen such a sight, Sire. Never in my life, and I am an Inquisitor.

'The murderer had taken his act to a climax. Literally according to Doctor Niall Ó'Glacáin. The death was a mercy. And the murder a conclusion of the work, one that is…was…much more extreme than …' My voice trailed-off. I cleared my throat and re-commenced,

'It is hard to conceive the mind that could do this to another human - and I an experienced Inquisitor. And yet, even the church has never stretched to these extremes.'

'You are an Inquisitor and you are to become mine own Inquisitor. Not the church's. Any loyalty that you held for that Pope… you need to forget. And forget completely if you wish…certain rewards.

Else you run the risk of become the first subject of my *new* Inquisitors investigation. Do I make myself clear.'

His eyes had turned a steely blue and I knew that the threat was real.

'Of course your highness.' I gulped as I answered.

✪

'And now Topcliffe I need to know your own thoughts on this murder. You have a suspect I believe this ... Holdem-Downe. You know this man?'

'Yes, Your Grace. I was at the Lincoln School with him.'

'Indeed...and Hotspur and the Younger Devereux boy too...and also the Waterton...girl...woman now?'

'Why yes, Your Grace...'

'Hotspur is a loyal dog, we like him well. Tell us of this younger Devereux - his brothers died in our cause. He is working for our agent Strix now, I believe. We know the father and the mother too. Their family has suffered greatly. That is the sad lot of some. I feel for the young man. Don't you Piers?'

'Indeed Your Grace...lovers parting....such sweet sorrow.' His fingers played a long mazy lick on the mandolin.

'Thomas is a fine young man sire, much clever than he pretends to be. We have a file on the whole family. They are staunch supporters of the crown. He is a good soldier, as are his father and brothers. I mean brother, two dying at Rouen, so recently. He has experience in the Crusades and the Scottish war. He fought for you at Bannockburn, Sire. I like him.' I said honestly.

'Those damned Templars! We could have won if Lancaster had turned up and those damned Templars had stayed in the Holy Land!' Edward threw a bowl of nuts across the room. They danced like marbles on the tiled floor. Several retainers scrambled to collect them. The madness left his brow and was almost immediately replaced by a soft smile. Still I saw a smouldering hate in his eyes. He recommenced the conversation as if nothing had occurred.

'And the woman? She is…well, another problem entirely.

I am concerned that the young Devereux should be so intoxicated with her. I don't like it. I don't like her. Which means I distrust him…still both Strix and Dee speak well of him too,' the King said. Gaveston looked at him with dark eyes and a secret smile spread across both their faces.

'Let us just say that, we have will make our arrangements concerning the Lady Waterton and her like…these Freethinkers.' The King paused and, selecting an apple from a different bowl at his elbow, took a huge, crunching bite.

'However…' he said through the mouthful,

'I do believe it would be prudent if this Holden-Downe was to…shall we say…confess…to this dreadful murder of the esteemed professor.' He devoured the apple completely.

'I understand he has slipped your net?'

'Yes your grace.' I gulped, '…but I am confident that we will apprehend him soon. I have the ports under surveillance and we are searching the homes of his friends…'

'Forget the ports my dear man. You should concentrate your efforts closer to hand. Have you been to Lincoln recently?'

'To the school, Your Grace?' I asked bewildered.

'To Stowe Abbey.' said Gaveston with a smile and a

strum on the mandolin.

'Holdem-Downe's father is there. Geoffrey Plantagenet, the Bishop of Lincoln. The illegitimate son of an illegitimate son. The only grandson of Henry FitzEmpress. If this young man was hung as the murderer not only would we end the speculation, the rumours, the fear…but we would also deal a might blow to our political enemies. Plantagenet and Church both!' Edward said triumphantly.

'A consummation devoutly to be wished!' Gaveston said as he finished his mandolin chord progression with a stylish blues ending lick in the key of 'G.'

37

The Witch Finder.

King Edward of Caernarfon, Piers Gaveston and the royal court are congregated for the feast of Lammas which they will celebrate at Nottingham Castle, NG1 6EL. Amongst those summoned to appear before the court are Mathew Hopkins, The Witchfinder General.

'Your Highness, presenting…a gentleman…' the court usher announced in his soupy voice, coughing lightly, as if he was not sure about the latter part of his last statement being at all true.

'Mister…Matthew Hopkins, esquire.' he finished his announcement.

Piers and I watched as the man, younger than I had expected, approached. He stopped five paces away and made his bow. He flourished his hat extravagantly and bent low. He looked quite ungainly when he made the manoeuvre, for he was tall and thin, yet a well muscled man. Much the same age as Piers and I, in his mid-twenties, and he had the look of one who practises often at the pell, the look of someone who had seen military action.

His cloak was a black satin, and he wore a plain leather gambeson, again black in colour, and covered with metal strips and studs. His longsword sat snuggly at his hip. It had a red dragon head, and for a moment the black eyes of the dragon shone white hot, like the coals of a deep fire.

'Ah Hopkins,' I said addressing him smoothly.

'I have been hearing of your exploits in Essex. It is said that you are hunting witches.'

'Your Highness…that word should have reached you is fantastic to my mind. The Gods must have a hand in this…how not?' he said again, bowing his head. His eyes studied my feet studiously.

'*Pourquoi oui mon ami, comment réalisez-vous votre travail?*' Piers asked him. Hopkins looked dumbfounded and his eyes begged for the comprehension, that his ears could not provide.

'My friend, Piers…the Earl of Cornwall…wishes to know how you go about your…work?' I explained to him. He smiled enthusiastically and began his story.

'Your Highness…it is my calling. My father was man of the Gods, the Vicar of St John's in Great Denham, near Bedford, in the shire of that name. And I was trained in the teaching of the King's scriptures from an early age.' He paused and a look of conviction came into his jet black eyes. He continued with a renewed confidence.

'I have also served Your Grace's father, the late king…in his campaigns in Scotland and Wales. We did the work of the Gods, bring Christian ideology to those heathen tribes. Slaying the evil druids. And our swords shone a holy red.' He paused for a small moment before continuing with zeal;

'Still, there is more work to do for my disciples and I. So much more. For the work of the Gods is never finished.'

His eyes were truly blazing as he uttered the last sentence and I knew we had found our man.

'You would make a good Templar, my dear man,' I said plainly.

'The Templars…' he paused for a moment as if considering the idea;

'Their work is in the heathen lands. And a true calling it is but they are so Popeish. I serve your Grace's Gods. And there is also work to be done here. We must tend to our own garden. If we wish to prosper, we need to till the soil…and root out the evil there. For the sinful do multiply with their fornication… they spread like very weeds. And they will proliferate. Their sins choking our crops, bringing down damnation, ruin, and famine upon us.'

Piers whispered to me softly;

'*Voici un homme qui mène une croisade dans son coeur!*'

My friend says '*that you are a man who carries a crusade in your heart*' I translated for him, before continuing.

'They say that, in your recent campaign, you have dispatched twenty and three of these heathen women.

Tell me Hopkins, how do you feel about The Freethinkers? How do *our* Gods feel about them?' I asked him. Piers and I share a look. We both watched him closely as he replied.

'For those women who practise witchcraft, those idol worshipers, the daughters of demons, those with wild heretical ideas…these so called freethinkers…their fate shall be cataclysmic…and they can not save themselves. For they will be submitted to the flames…and a fiery death. And a lake of burning sulphur awaits them in the end. They shall have no resistance to the tongues of the inferno. It shall constantly lick at them. And their soul will know no rest. And I…my holy work…is to speed them on their way.'

'And what of those…those who reside in these wild norths…North of the Gap. You got the King's direction on that matter?' Piers asked him in the jilted, stumbling, manner that he sometimes employs when he seeks to mis-direct people as to his real intelligence.

'I did Your Grace. And I must say that I feel that there resides a woman who is heathen to the core. We, Stearne and my warriors, relish the opportunity to crusade in that hotbed of heathens. A truly forsaken region. For there is no end to the work of Gods.' stated Hopkins crossing himself.

Piers nodded, and I smiled in agreement

38

A Visit To The Library

Sir Thomas Devereux; is in his rooms above the emporium of Messrs Camden and Sons, by royal warrant and appointment to his gracious majesty Edward II, Royal Astronomers, Astrologers, Cartographers, Chart Makers, Horologist, Navigators, Oikouménê, Scribists, and who are of the Worshipful Company of Painter-Stainers and Sporting Bookmakers, which are situated in Neal's Yard, London, WC2H 9DP.

At the request of his mysterious friend Strix he is continuing his investigation into the strange murder of Professor Witherspoon, and its tenuous connection to Old Cathy.

Summertime in London can sometimes surprise you. We have been having a torrent of rain recently but, as August dawned, the weather changed for the better and that which should have arrived in the Languedoc or España, had unexpectedly turned up in the capital instead. The sun was smiling, the air was fresh, and there was no sign in the sky of those rain clouds or *Flemish* weather as we call it, which is our usual lot.

I had decided that a walk would do me good. I could use the exercise to help lose some of that excess weight that Yvette had mentioned. I'm afraid that my recent retirement from military service, and

an over indulgence in Yvette's cooking, had brought
me up to something approaching maximum capacity. And so it was that I made my way along Shaftesbury Avenue, on towards Bloomsbury, across Russell
Square and north, to the Great Library.

There was about ten minutes to go until the start
of the show and I decided to peruse one or two of
the paintings hanging on the walls. I won't go into
details about the art on display. Suffice to say that
whilst studying it, two things grabbed my attention.

Both of them were female, and beautiful.

The first was Young Bess. We call her Young Bess,
en famille, as she is my mother's younger cousin,
which makes her my cousin-aunt. She is in reality of
course, Her Grace, Princess of the bloode, Elisabeth,
and she is only twenty or so moons older than me.
There had been some talk of a match between us,
but a small problem had occurred. My derivation I
presume, and well…that obviously proved to be an
obstacle, which was a shame, as we had always been
good friends. She was one of the few well educated
women that I knew. If she was less royal, I'm sure
she would have been a freethinker. I could see her
and Yvette getting along like a house of fire. They
would both love bullying me for a start.

'Hello Young Bess.' I said to her after the courtly
pleasantries had been delivered and her escorts had
backed away to give us some privacy.

'Oh Thom! How nice to see you. You seemed to
have recovered well from your injuries. Have you
given up the chainmail now? And what of the Templars?' She flashed her blue green eyes at me and
smiled, her red hair bouncing around her shoulders
as we walked towards the main hall, chatting like
the old friends that we were.

'Tell me Thom, do you still see that northern girl? I
only ask out of politeness. You know your mother is

always pushing you onto me. I suppose if …'

'Yes, I know.' I said hurriedly;

'She wants me to marry. But I'm afraid that being a spare…the fourth son and all that, and being…well… Oh!' I stopped my eyes widening. I was so used to their being four sons.

'Yes, I didn't know your brothers well but I was so sorry to hear of their deaths. The Franks need a decent thrashing.' The lights in her eyes flashed intensely.

'I suppose their death changes things. I mean you are second in line now, are you not? Behind your father and Robert.' I took her meaning immediately.

'You mean mother has been speaking with you again? Already?' She nodded and smiled at me, looping her arm through mine as we strolled along the corridor.

'Yes. She has. Would you hate the match so much? You know… I *am* considering you.' She asked the question that had hung between us for the best part of a year now. She had looked me directly in the eye and I felt the colour flooding my face. She blushed also and hit me, not so gently, on the arm. We must have looked like the twin planets of Red Mars.

'I…I love Yvette.' My eyes dropped from hers.

'I realise that it is doomed. And that mother is totally opposed to the relationship. Still…'

Bess held me close for a moment, a small hug, and then taking a small step back she said;

'Above all: to thine own self be true. And it must follow, as the night follows the day, thou canst not then be false to thine own heart,' she quoted.

'See…I do read your work!' She smiled at me and I did feel a certain emotion begin to rise.

'I can't say that I am surprised. I am a little disappointed too. A girl likes to think that she can bowl a young man over, you know! Just to be clear, because

I feel this is important…I would look at the proposition with a glad heart. When I am to marry, I would like it to be to someone that I like…admire even.' She leaned in and kissed me softly. It was a sweet moment.

'A breath, a frothy effervescence of fleeting joy,' I said to her. And I meant it. She laughed.

'John Dee has always expressed the opinion to me, that you have a remarkable destiny. He thinks you will be a great man, you know.' Bess continued.

'What - really? You're not confusing me with someone else are you? I do hope he's not feeling ill.'

She laughed again, and her eyes flashed at me, like a girl's eyes do.

'So, what are you doing here?' she inquired.

'I thought I would attend the lecture on Sinology.' I replied.

'Sinology, really…you?' She looked at me oddly;

'You know, John may be right. I *too* am attending that lecture. You can accompany me,' she said easily, like one who is accustomed to giving commands. And, of course, who can refuse a princess?

'Do you know who is delivering the lecture?' I asked absently.

'Yes, it's a Professor from Hong Kong University called Professor Xai. He's in the city with the Celestial Trade Envoy, and has stood in for the late Professor Witherspoon, who was murdered last week, in that Cambridge sex scandal,' she said, as we made our way to the hall.

'Yes, poor old Withers.' I said.

'Did you know him? Oh, tell me all about it…the scandal.'

'Oh yes, I knew *of* him, an acquaintance only I stress. We had barely been introduced before he was murdered. Still, it is a bad business.

'I am afraid that life is not sacred any more. He was

attacked in his home you know. Let this be a lesson to you, Young Bess - at any moment the cruel hand of fate can open a door, and death may walk in,' I preached to her.

Now, I don't know if you believe in fate but sometimes the oddest things do happened. I had made my warning just as we had reached the top of the stairs and were walking slowly towards the door of the reading room, when what do you think happened?

The door opened, and death walked in!

Now you probably don't believe me, and I must admit to not trusting the feelings that I felt myself, but I wouldn't have been surprised if an orchestra had struck up and provided theme music for the entrance. The person who walked through the door was the second of the beautiful women that I encountered that morning. And I must say that, when the Gods made this beauty, well…let's just say that they had really cracked on. She was tallish, about my height, very thin, and of Celestial appearance, and she wore the most beautiful of silk dresses that I have ever seen.

'Oh, what a beautiful dress,' said Young Bess, which just goes to prove that my judgment in these matters cannot be far off the mark. Still, she did send a chill down my spine, and also in to my very braies. I smiled to myself as I thought about the recent Boxer uprisings we had heard about in Old Cathay.

39

Professor Xia's Lecture

Sir Thomas Devereux; is at the Great Library, London, NW1 2DB, to attend the lecture on Sinology, where he has met his mother's relative and close friend, Bess Tudor.

We were seated in the reading room, when a small man with a long beard stood up on the podium and started to address the ensemble. He sprouted on about; 'How welcome we all where...' before saying, '...and how pleased the society were to see us...' and '...of course, how the society, and everyone here, he felt sure, would like to offer their most sincere sympathy to the family of the late Professor Witherspoon...' for a few minutes.

'He can't have known the chap very well,' I whispered to Bess, who thumped me in the ribs with her elbow this time. Still, he continued;

'...it was a pleasure, and again, I feel quite sure that you would agree, for the Society of Sinology, to be able to be addressed...by the extremely well dressed Sinophile.' Here he laughed. So did one or two other feeble brained types who were sat near the front. Obviously, they had all gone to university together, somewhere like Oxford, or maybe even Durham.

'...And with no further ado, he took great pleasure in inviting Professor Xia, from the University of Honk Kong, who will address the meeting.'

Well, it's not very often that you could knock me down with a feather. But I do believe that if you had tried at that very moment, you would have had unprecedented success. It seems that there had been some sort of mistake. For the program definitely stated that Professor Xia would address the meeting, and that *he* was in the capital as part of the Celestial Trade Envoy from Old Cathay, and by pure coincidence, was available to, at very short notice… replace the terminally late Professor Witherspoon.

The mistake was evident. The Professor Xia from the University of Hong Kong was a woman, and not just any woman, but indeed the same woman who had exited through the doors as Young Bess and I had reached them.

Professor Xia stood quite effectively on the small podium at the front of the room and addressed the gathering in a clear voice. Her accent was a strange mixture of Celestial English and that perfect English, which is only spoken by the people of the ministry, mother-in laws, and girls who play hockey. She held the audience spellbound as she expounded her theories about the T'Ang dynasty.

She explained that she had been very excited by Professor Witherspoon's findings. And, although she could not agree with all of his conclusions, she felt that several were largely in agreement with the very theories she herself had announced only the previous month.

In particular, the evidence of the coloured etchings on the vase, which were by far the most important factual evidence that had been produced in the last half century. In fact, since her late father had indeed explained and documented the finds at Ch'Ang- An in Shaan Xi. In particular, she went on to explain how it related to the story of

Feng Tai Wu...

A story that was very common in the Celestial Empire but was thought, except by a few, to be pure fantasy. It was the story concerning the whereabouts of a fantastic treasure. A treasure that had been buried during the reign of the Emperor Li Tsu, the last scion of the T'Ang dynasty. Once or twice it was alleged that pieces of the treasure had come to light, and they fetched fantastical prices but the finders, and indeed the buyers, had all died mysteriously only days after the treasure had come into their possession, and the treasure had again disappeared, only to be lost in the mists of time.

'The legend of Emperor Li Tsu was evil, and the curse of the treasure was death.' Professor Xia paused for effect. This caused quite a stir amongst the doublets and cloaks of the Sinologists, as I'm sure you can imagine. But everyone loves a treasure story, especially when it is told by a beautiful young lady.

Professor Xia went on to explain that most of the archaeological finds in Far Cathay had been before the Empire's and Far East Company's Opium Wars. Still, now that there was an established, if uneasy, peace treaty in place, there seemed to be a more open channel of communication. It was her greatest ambition to carry on the work of her late father in the excavation of the ruins in and around the city of Ch'Ang- An.

The rest of her lecture was indeed about the work that her father had undertaken in and around that ancient city. And although of great interest, I'm sure, it would be far easier for you to read her book;

*'The Secrets of Old Cathay; Archaeol-
ogy and Myth.'
By Professor M. Xia*

Published by Johanssons of Bethnal Green, London. E2 7ES

However, for those of you who are unable to acquire a copy of Professor Xia's work. I shall précis it for you:

The general story is of an Emperor called Li Tsu, the last scion of the house of T'Ang. He came to power about nine hundred years ago and at a banquet that lasted four days, held to celebrate his ascendancy by his gweilo warlord, the warlord poisoned all of Li Tsu's brothers. He did this so as to secure a peaceful and un-challenged reign. However, the inner story or subtext as she called it, held a secret. It was a kind of secret message, a code, with hidden clues, that may or may not lead to the treasure.

✪

After the lecture had finished there was an informal lunch.

'Professor Xia was quite dismissive of Witherspoon's theories, don't you think? I couldn't help but think we didn't get the whole story from her,' Young Bess said to me.

'Perhaps I should go and ask her a few questions.' I suggested.

I thought it an interesting idea - you never know where it may lead.

'You had better hurry,' replied Bess, giving me a look that seemed to penetrate, as it were.

'She's just leaving.' And she pointed out of the window with a cucumber sandwich.

I put down my platter and moved closer to the window. Young Bess linked her arm through mine, holding me closely, and leaned her head on my shoulder. We were just in time to see Professor Xia climb into a fine carriage pulled by six midnight black horses. And, with a crack of the whip, it sped off eastwards, towards Limehouse.

'I think I will get a copy of old Withers' thesis. Just for interest you know,' I told her.

40

Tales From The River Bank

Sir Thomas Devereux; is in his rooms above the emporium of Messrs Camden and Sons, by royal warrant and appointment to his gracious majesty Edward II, Royal Astronomers, Astrologers, Cartographers, Chart Makers, Horologist, Navigators, Oikouménê, Scribists, and who are of the Worshipful Company of Painter-Stainers and Sporting Bookmakers, which are situated in Neal's Yard, London, WC2H 9DP.

It was the day after the lecture at the library and I was to meet with Strix and then John Dee later that day. I currently sat at the scribing table, pretending to work on one of my chronicles, dreaming of my sweet Yvette, and, all the while, thoughts of Witherspoon's murder kept drifting through my mind, and I knew that I would have to start the search for that barge girl. Robyn, tomorrow.

Mr. Eddie 'Cleanhead' Vinson was relating one of his epic stories of urban life deep within the American Free States, in which he; *'Went in the front door... but had to take the back door out!'* And was, by all accounts, most grateful for his life, as several crossbow quarrels struck the surrounding walls, and his lover's husband, a man of whose existence he had been blissfully unaware, screamed after him down some shabby alley deep in a squalid neighbourhood of a city somewhere in the Colonies. I do love the passion of such lyrics.

Now, just as Eddie's story was unfolding, I found on an inner page of *The Tears of Hermes* an interesting story about a fisherman of greater London Town. It seem that this fisherman was idling away his hours, as is his pleasure, in the neighbourhood of the River Ember, hard by East Molesey, when to his great surprise, he landed himself quite the largest catch of his life. Not only does the catch outweigh any previous prize, it seemed that it had once walked and breathed as men will do.

What a predicament! Here is a poor wagon master, taking his leisure, and simply out to supply himself with his evening supper when, to his surprise, a gentleman of celestial appearance comes to take a bite, as they say.

Not quite the 'take away' that he would have ordered, one presumes.

Well, the Dibble were called, and the pamphleteers and broadsheets come and interview the fisherman, and the story unfolds. It appears that the celestial had not been taking the waters purely for the benefit of his health and ,insofar as the Dibble are concerned, possibly not of his own volition.

Of course, the officials have no idea of the identity of the bathing celestial, save that on his right arm was a tattoo of a red dragon.

'The fisherman, Robert of Winslowe [43], of The Angel Inn, Nightingale Lane, Balham, SW12 9DU, had suffered no ill effects from consuming his catches' wrote Manus O'Heron.

By now, the wax cylinder has moved on to Big Mama Thornton who is watching the rain through her window, when the doorbell rings.

Not Big Mama's door bell, my doorbell. I say rings but it really whistles, and I call it a bell, but I suppose it is really a type of thing-y. You know the type of thing-y, that sends a dried pea around a thing-y somehow, and it lets out a shrill whistle. They have the same thing on ships I understand.

Anyway what happens is that the person on the outside blows into the tube, and inside the whistle sounds, and you take the stopper out of the tube, and speaking into your end say '*Hello.*'And they on the outside say '*It's me.*' And you, still on the inside, say '*Oh, come up.*' And you pull the lever, which slides the cogs, which moves the lock, which gives them access, at the outer door below.

Well as I say the doorbell gave off its merry whistle, so I went over and spoke into the tube.

'Hello.'

'Oh hello, Thom, it's me, Bess. Can I speak with you for a few moments?' asked the voice on the outside.

'Of course, Your Grace,' said I, ever the gentleman.

'Please take several. Do come on up. It's the black door on the second floor.' I suppose I could have said the top floor or even the penthouse but you take your choice and today second floor seemed about right as there are only the two.

Well, by the time I had turned off my stereo, and stashed some contraband in its hiding place, Young Bess was waiting on the mat, as I've heard Marlowe express it.

'Good evening, Your Grace, you young thing you,' I said as I bowed to her with a flurry of my hand.

'How nice to see you. Please, do come in.'

She nodded to her guards who stood at the door, and then she stepped inside.

'Please let me take your cloak. Will you sit? Would you like some of my special, newly smuggled, highly illicit coffee?' I asked her.

'Oh, yes please. If I may. That's what I love so much about you Thom. You treat me like I am a normal person,' came her *too* quick reply.

Now call me a fuddy-duddy but Young Bess did not seem quite herself.

'You seem on edge my dear Bess - what on earth is wrong?' I asked her as I placed the coffee on the table between the two low couches and took a seat opposite her.

'Well I'm not quite sure. I am quite at odds with myself. It's Doctor Dee. He wrote me such a strange letter.'

I raised an eyebrow thinking; *'He does that all the time. What can be so strange about this one?'*

She withdrew a parchment from the secret recesses of her gown and handed it to me. It was neatly folded and edged. I could still see the cracked wax that it held the impression of John's seal. Two circles that were within a mathematical symbol that looked somewhat like an elongated seven.

I knew that the symbol represented his eyes, that were always hidden, yet wakeful in her service. Somewhere in the cobweb laden recesses of my dim mind it struck a chord. It reminded me of something that I had seen recently but just couldn't place my finger upon.

Your Royal Highness,
Humbly pray I for your continued radiance,
a splendour for which we extol such divine
blessings.

And before we raise our eyes to the heavens,
illuminated by the contemplation of these
kabbalist mysteries, we should perceive very
exactly the constitution of our monad, as it
is shown to us, not only in the light but also
in life, and in nature.

For it discloses explicitly, by its inner move-
ment, the most secret mysteries of this phys-
ical analysis.

So humbly be it that I present to you upon
this day, the corollary allied to my labours,
both pursued and explored.

From said mysteries; I do conclude, that day
and date, and instance, are transmuted,
and do transmigrate by thirty and three
days in each year.
And thus do the days and the months, and
the years combine, coalesce, mingle, merge
and flux.

Tho' still the transmutations do become
more brisk. And we may perceive thus far,
that, the transmigrating, in said instances,
may enlarge 'til it will become not days, yet
years.

And still within the longitudes that do
encircle the blessed worlde, do these trans-
migrations intensify and proliferate until
such, we can contemplate, be that;

He, whom is not yet born,
may still walk upon this earth,
and live within this world,
and spread forth his seed.

I am forever your humble, obedient servant,
in faith and true in flesh and mind,

Doctor John Dee
ōō7

When I had finished reading, she looked at me
with those big green eyes of hers, and hesitated for a
moment before saying;
'I think he's disappeared.'

41

Fireball

***John Stearne;** the Witch Pricker and able assistant to Matthew Hopkins, the Witchfinder General, is with his employer and their men, at the Watermill, on the edge of the market town of Axholme, which stands on the borders of Nottinghamshire, Yorkshire, and Lincolnshire.*

It is the home of the evil woman, Lady Yvette Waterton [unmarried], a known freethinker; and necromancer.

'Burn, Lady Waterton. That is all I want - to see you burn!'

Mathew Hopkins, the Witchfinder General, laughed hysterically as I threw another firebrand and we watched it crash through the window of the watermill. I dismounted in the yard and passed my reins to one of Cartwright's men. The shouted phrase was the signal for us to begin our work, and we had laid the trap well.

The rear door of the mill, which led from the kitchen, was guarded by two of our men. They had a large stack of faggots ready piled up against it and soon it would be ablaze. There would be no escape from that route.

I smiled to myself.

'And wherefore it behoves a man to prevent the power of the devil, and the necromancer...so down goes the power of witchery!' I quoted as I set about my night's work.

'Do not worry Lady Waterton!' called the voice of Matthew Hopkins,

'I come to repay your kindness, and your hospitality! There will be no choice or chance with a *pricking* for you. The cards have been dealt and your hand is in! Aces and eights!' He laughed.

The other men had dismounted too, while one held the horses. We set about our task. I led two of them to the front door. We hammered at it with axes and finished the job simply with our shoulders.

'Burn the Witch!' shouted the General, as his horse spun, its terror-filled eyes reflecting the flames that had taken up on the thatch of the kitchen roof.

The door fell open on the second thrust of our shoulders. It did so with a dry, sharp, splintering, sound.

We moved in to the entrance hall with our firebrands, spilling the flames onto everything that would take a light. Tapestries, curtains, baskets, parchment, and books, all took alight with a mighty whoosh!

Before we could move beyond the door's immediate area, two massive dogs attacked us. I remembered that we had encountered these beasts upon our previous visit. They jumped at us. Mosley went down under one, as I drew my sword.

Nort lay into the other dog. His blade cut deep, right across the beast's back, drawing a blood-red slash down its flank. Then more dogs - smaller, hunting hounds they were, and perhaps ten or twelve of them - swarmed around us. They leaped, snarling and biting at my hands and balls. They seem to be devil possessed, and well they maybe. Her familiars. I crossed myself quickly.

'Jesu, give your servant strength!'

I pushed forward but stumbled, and then something that may have been a cat, leapt at my face. It scratched at me, digging its claws deep into my cheek. The oil in the pot jar that I held slopped about violently. It spilled down the front of my woollen gambeson and onto my legs. I cursed loudly as I flung it down the corridor, aiming to hit the witch before she disappeared through the open kitchen door. The smoke billowed madly but I saw that the flames had taken hold.

They instantly leapt upwards and I knew our job was done.

'Nort, carry Mosley and let us be out of here!' I shouted as the fire and smoke filled the small corridor. I watched absently, as a finger of flame dropped from the door to the floor. It stood for a moment like a naughty child caught with his hand in the biscuit jar, not knowing whether to stay or to run. Then it made its mind up.

It ran.

It ran straight towards me and leapt easily up from the floor to my boots and my leathers, and on to my gambeson and cloak. I patted at the flames with my hands, extinguishing them.

Then I saw the man Nort look at me, as he helped Mosley out of the door. His face told me all I needed to know. Horror flowed from his eyes.

I looked at my hands. The flames I had extinguished had burst back to life. They burned through the soft leather of my gloves. I staggered after the men, shouting for help. The flames reached my long hair and then my beard, and I smelt the burning singe of my whiskers, hot in my nostrils.

'*Water, I must get to the water*' was all I could think. I rushed outside, lighting my own way in the darkness of the night. I saw the men staring at me.

The General watched with a savage lust and, as I turned, I saw the boy monk leave the mill, staggering like myself.

Yet he was not on fire at all. A mist or vapour seemed to be following him as he went. His habit smouldered but the flames that did appear died just as quickly.

'*Jesu, help me now I pray!*' I shouted in my head, for I could feel my tongue was blistering.

I saw that one of the great dogs lay bleeding and the other was leaping up at Nort. As I staggered I could feel my burning flesh sticking to the leathers, and I could actually hear my skin blistering, bubbling, and popping, and the instant crackle of each of the hairs on my head as they sizzled away.

'You will never take me alive!' I heard the witch shout.

Then the wind blew sharply, and for a moment the flames died down I could see the mill as it roared ferociously. I could hear the screams of the witch. She stood cloaked by the kitchen window. The flames danced around her, consuming her entirely, and I smiled.

'*The freethinker, the evil base woman, necromancer!*'

Her magic and conjuring would not save her now. Her screams could be heard filling the night with terror, and I knew our work was done.

'*Where is your curse now witch?*' I screamed silently at her.

And there, mounted on his black mare, there sat the General. Matthew Hopkins, my friend and companion, we were holy warriors together.

I could see his eyes smiling at me. A sad smile for sure, but soon he laughed. And I laughed with him, as the fire took hold of the mill.

Then the lull passed, and the flames flared up more savagely than ever before and I heard a whoosh.
All I could see was red, and orange, and yellow, and white. I staggered forward, hearing only dogs bark-

ing and the shouts of men and the sweet sputter of roasting meat. It smelled good too.

I no longer saw much of anything. I felt the pain. A fresh agony - I tried to scream but my mouth would not move. I could feel my tongue bursting open,as the flame was sucked through my chest and into my lungs.

'And the tongue is aflame of the fire. It is a whole world of wickedness, corrupting my entire body. It defileth my whole life, it burns with flame, for it was set on fire by hell itself!'

A Dangerous Man

Sir Thomas Devereux; *is meeting with the Mysterious Strix at the Nellie Dean, which stands on a small corner of Dean Street and Carlisle Street, Soho, London. W1D 3SU*

'They have him!' I shouted as I charged in to the small front room of the Nellie Dean.

'It's here! All over *'The Tears.'* I said thrusting the newsheet into my friend's face. Strix was infinitely more composed, as is his style. He gave me that hard, steely eyed, look that he sometimes gives to people and slowly took the newsheet from under his nose and placed it on the table. I sat down next to him, my back to the wall. Subdued, I ordered a round of beers from the blonde Nellie as she approached us with her smile and a wink.

'I am well aware that they have apprehended young Holdem-Downe…A dangerous man! Bah! A *Dangerous Fool* more like.

'We both know that this is a travesty,' he said, picking up *The Tears* and throwing it back upon the table. Several people glanced at us. Quickly, and without saying a word, they looked away again, attending to to their own business. Still, they had noticed.

'A show…like one of those play-acting things you seem to becoming involved in writing. This could be a plot for your next endeavours…or even one of Marlowe's fantasies,' he said with a sneer.

'And I believed that you like Marlowe!' I thought. I

could tell he was unhappy. Lightning seemed to be dancing in the inky recesses of his eyes, and the beginnings of a dark cloud appeared to be forming just above his eyebrows and slightly to the right.

'You feel they have the wrong man, what?' I said, stating the obvious.

'Obviously they have the wrong man! It is a show! As I say…playacting. We know that this boy is not the murderer that we are looking for. Still, it does draw the attention of the crowd and…' He paused and raised his glass giving his usual toast when in public;

'The King.'

I joined him, and waited for the great man to recommence his oration.

'There will, of course, be a progression. He will be brought, in chains, from Lincoln to London. Like the mighty Vercingetorix. The public will vent their collective anger as he is dragged across the country. And that very anger will unite the kingdom. Clever.'

> *'Man united,*
> *Forming a single nation,*
> *Animated by a common spirit,*
> *Can defy the Universe.'*

I quoted, remembering the intentional misquote of the stanza. One that we always found so humorous in my dear old school days.

'Did you see what I did there; Man United? They Beat The Wednesday 32 -19 last week. However I am not sure about these new *Sheffield Rules*. 'Kicking Off' at some hypothetical spot in the middle…what *is* the point?'

Strix shook his head in disgust at my feeble brained

joviality and swift change of subject. He drank more beer whilst he readied his thoughts. I watched as the lightning in his eyes ceased to spark and the cloud above his right eyebrow almost dissolved completely, just as a small smile traced the outline of his mouth. Of course it was well hidden behind his dark beard. Still, I knew it was there.

'You play the fool to ease my mood. It was well intended…it was well done. You can be the most personable damned fool.' And he did now smile, if only for the moment.

'Was that a compliment…from Strix?' I wondered.

'There will be a show trial, at which no doubt, your friend Soapy will preside and finally the White Tower, as his rank entitles him.

'Still…no, I think mayhap not…too many high ranking prisoners at the moment, and the Tower is filling up.

'No…it is more probable that the King will seek to pour still further humiliation upon the Plantagenets, as he has his prisoner dragged to Canterbury and the Whitehouse Cage. Eh? The Oubliette. Before a very public execution…' Strix paused and finished his beer.

'Come! His Grace expects us to continue with our own line of enquiry. There *is* a dangerous man to find. We still have work to do. You have heard that John Dee has gone missing?'

The Season of the Witch

Sir Thomas Devereux; is about his daily chores and is returning from Covent Garden market to his apartment in Neal's Yard, London, WC2H 9DP.

'When I look out the window
Many sights to see
And when I look out the window
So many people to be
That's it's strange
So strange
Some other cat lookin' over
His shoulder at me
And he is strange

Must be the season of the witch'

The song ended abruptly, as the plod pushed the hurdy-gurdy man roughly to the ground and kicked him hard in the stomach. He fell into the deep muddy puddle just on the corner of Short's Gardens and Drury Lane and, at that moment, to show the Gods' displeasure the skies darkened and a great crack of thunder split the air.

This, however, did not help the hurdy-gurdy man at all as the plod continued to kick him relentlessly. I rushed over and shouted at them, my hand grabbing at my sword hilt and pulling.

'Stop in the name of the Gods. Leave the fellow be!' I said, brandishing Red Feather.

'Away with you little Lord-ling,' said the big, tall, mean looking plod, lifting his whistle to his lips and blowing a sharp shrill blast. He had faced a blade before.

'Away I say…or you too will spend the night at His Majesty's pleasure. Musicians are not allowed outside of the designated performance areas now and he knows it.'

They kicked him some more and just as I was about to have at them a hand clutched at my shoulder. More officers piled into the street. The hand had a voice, which said softly in my ear;

'Strix, Nellie Dean, third bell, dog watch.'

A small, bulky package was shoved into my hand. And then he was gone. I searched around for him but the urchin had vanished; *Like an evil spirit at the dawn of day,* I thought as I took a quick look at the package he had pressed into my hand.

It was yellow parchment, fastened with red ribbon and wax. The sealing wax held the image of a long-tailed bird and my heart leapt as I recognised whose seal it was. I smiled a secret smile, and felt my cock stiffen just at the thought of her. I kissed it lovingly before stuffing it into a pocket deep within my cloak, and stood back and watched as the plod carried the hurdy-gurdy man off, throwing him roughly into the back of the Black Maria.

'It's Clink Street for you,' he snarled.

Two of them threw the instrument on top of his broken and bleeding body. The street urchins dashed and fought to collect the few coppers that the man had left in his damp, muddy cap.

The tall plod flexed his muscles, gave me a hard stare and beat his palm with his cudgel. I could see the malice in his eyes and knew he wished that he could throw me into that Black Maria too. Still rank does have some privileges, and he dare not touch me without further provocation. And I longed to give him so much provocation. So much provocation that it hurt. I stared back at him, just daring him to make a move.

In my mind I could see Red Feather licking his blood, like a cat laps at milk. Instead I stared him down and squeezed the hilt of Red Feather hard, until it hurt. Marlowe sped around the corner from Neal's Yard and nearly barged into me, as he shouted;

'Dev! Oh Dev, I've been looking for you, I must have been banging on your door for the past year.'

He exaggerated, but then again he exaggerated about everything, as playwrights always do.

'I'm not in…' I said harshly, still seething as I watched the Black Maria head off around the corner. The plod departed with it. I looked down, sadly, at the muddy puddle and watched as it turned a muddier dark pink.

'Dev. The news!'

The lightning bolt flashed a frightful whipcrack that spit and fizzled so brightly that I was blinded for a moment and then an almighty sizzle flashed, as Thor's powerbolt struck the cobbles. The thunder bellowed a shattering roar, like a thousand drums being beaten at the same time, and the lightning whip sounded like a great oak tree had splintered.

It was like nothing I had ever experienced - so loud that it felt like the Gods were tearing the world asunder.

It began to rain. Such a rain. A rain that bounced down to the earth. A harsh relentless rain. A rain without mercy. It fell so hard, that the drops bounced back upwards as high as my knees. I looked at Marlowe and saw the pain and the sorrow in his wide dark eyes. One long, silent, glance, in the pounding rain. And I knew…

And then my tears also poured.

Disclaimer

This novel is a work of fiction which takes place in a fantasy world. A substantial amount of imagination and creativity has been employed to ensure that any similarity between names, characters, businesses, places, events, incidents, actual persons, alive or dead, in your world are completely and purely coincidental.

More Information

More information on the Alchemy Series, The Great Book of Alchemy, the 5th Worlde Sagas and other related matter is available at the website.

http://www.5thworlde.com

&

http:// greatbookofalchemy.com